Chocolate Kiss of Death

A Willow Crier Cozy Mystery

Book 6

Lilly York

Chocolate Kiss of Death

A Willow Crier Cozy Mystery

Book 6

Cover Design: Jonna Feavel
40daygraphics.com

Illustrations: Ben Gerhards

Interior Layout: Daniel Mawhinney
40daypublishing.com

Published by: Wide Awake Books
wideawakebooks.com

Also available in eBook publication

Printed in the United States of America

Get your free short story!

Grandpa Goes Missing

Find out what happened to bring Willow down to
Oklahoma in the first place.
Be the first in line to read Lilly York's latest books, get
extra recipes from Willow's kitchen, get 'sneak peeks'
on works-in-progress, receive special offers and so
much more…
FREE short story only available here!

www.lillyyork.com/shortstory

Get yours today!

Chapter 1

Willow looked at herself in the full-length mirror. She turned in a circle, admiring the svelte person staring back. She had started carb cycling and for her, it was working. She liked every kind of food and she only got a free day once a week. There were weeks she lived for those free days but she could stay strong in-between, most of the time.

She walked around the room. The caterers did a lovely job. They were still finishing up the last-minute touches. The guests would be arriving in couple of hours. She had wanted a few minutes alone with her thoughts. The photo albums of the kids were on the gift table. She glanced through Embry's— stopping on photographs that brought strong memories. Some made her smile, some gave her pause. Her newborn picture. She didn't cry. She looked around curious and nosy—traits that remained all through her life and would probably carry her through to the end.

Her preschool picture with her frog backpack. That was the first time of many she made Willow cry. She didn't want Willow walking her into school. What four-year-old does that? She wanted to walk in by herself without her mother. Willow shook her head. Independence, sometimes referred to as stubbornness, also stuck to her like glue.

Willow flipped through the school years landing on her high school graduation. The little girl grew up to be a beautiful young woman. Willow couldn't be more proud of her. She started college then decided to wait and figure out what she wanted to do with her life. She decided, and it had nothing to do with a college education. She was going to be a wife and a mother. Willow smiled. She remembered her daughter's description of the house she would live in—in the country, across from Willow's, with a creek and a bridge separating them so she could bring her children over whenever she needed a babysitter. Willow tried to remind Embry of that promise to no avail. Her daughter had grown up and her dreams had grown up too.

Willow stopped at her engagement picture. Marshall's face glowed. The love he had for her daughter would last a lifetime. She thought about her own mistakes and thanked God her daughter hadn't made the same. Sure, she'd experience pain, but she would also know true love and happiness.

The doorbell interrupted Willow's walk-through time. She glanced at her watch. Whoever it is, was way too early. She let everyone know, even Steve, she wanted a little time by herself before anyone arrived. Otherwise her mascara would be sure to run. She had no plans to put her make up on until the last minute—perhaps she would spend her tears by then. Clover growled at the door, waiting to protect Willow from danger.

She opened the door, met her own past face to face, then slammed it. The doorbell rang again. She re-opened it. "What do you want?"

"Nice welcome for a guy you haven't seen in, what, over 20 years?"

"I could stand another 20 if you don't mind. You can leave now." She tried to close the door but he inserted his foot before it closed. Too bad she didn't have her gun on her. She could claim intruder and shoot the jerk.

The dog barked, her hair standing on end.

"Again, I ask, what do you want?"

He glanced nervously at the dog. Good, she thought, he should be afraid, very afraid.

"I want to talk. Is that so much to ask? Our daughter is engaged and going to be married. I thought a civil conversation might be in order."

"How do you know she's engaged?"

His face contorted into a superior, know it all look she remembered only too well. "She told me. How do you think?"

He was full of himself. And proud. Why, she had no idea. "We both know you're not here because of Embry. You've never been here for her. What do you really want?"

He reached out and caressed her cheek before she realized what he was doing. "I think we should give it another go. You know, for Embry's sake."

"Give what a go? You can't mean—a relationship?" Borrowing a phrase from her daughter she added, "Are you freaking kidding me?" She paused. "Oh, I get it. You heard I've inherited money. I noticed you didn't show up on my doorstep when you could have been taken to court for child support. Just so you know, I can still take you to court. Let's see…18 years of child support…you probably owe about a half a million with interest? Give or take?"

His cockiness disappeared. "Hey. I'm just here because Embry asked me to come. That's it. I don't want anything from you."

"The party doesn't start until six. Come back then." She ushered him out the door then picked up the phone and called Embry. No answer. Willow slammed the phone, well, she slammed the phone in her head. She missed house phones that had a nice base you could actually slam the receiver into. Cell phones were kind of hard to slam. You could only push the little button so hard without jamming your finger. She sure missed the good ole' days. Sometimes.

She paced back and forth. Paced might be too tempered, stomped was more like it. Clover found a corner and covered her head with her paws.

Embry wasn't answering her phone. Willow could only leave so many voicemails and still be considered sane. Although she supposed it didn't really matter if her daughter considered her to be sane. At least until she tried to have her committed to gain control of her assets. Not that Embry would ever do such a thing. At least Willow hoped she wouldn't.

She punched in Steve's number. She had to talk to someone. He answered on the first ring and she immediately erupted, telling him everything that happened. And when she finished, she burst out in tears. The only thing she heard on the other end of the line was, "I'll be right over."

A few minutes later she was crying on his shoulder. "I told you he wasn't an issue. Now he's back." She sniffled. "I tried to call Embry. She isn't answering. The man hasn't paid a single dime in child support, he's never been there for her, why would she call him?"

Steve ran his hand over her hair. "He's her dad. This is a once in a lifetime moment for her. Every child holds out that somehow, someway, even when all the evidence points elsewhere, the absent parent will whisk into their lives and suddenly become everything they have missed out on. Even grown kids hope. Even Embry wants a dad."

"How did you get to be so smart on parenting?" What she really wanted to say was, until you have kids, stuff it. But she didn't go there.

"Remember, I work at the shelter every week. I still volunteer and work with kids who are being raised without one, and sometimes two, parents. Every single one of them dream they'll be reunited someday. Embry isn't the exception."

"I know she said she was going to call him but I thought she might have backed out—that she wouldn't go through with it. And why wouldn't she tell me? I have 50 people coming over in less than an hour and I'm a mess. I could have been better prepared."

"Honey, she did try to tell you. You wouldn't listen."

Willow's eyebrows furrowed.

"I'm not trying to be mean. I'm just reminding you—your daughter did tell you."

Willow took a few deep breaths and dabbed her eyes with a tissue. "You're right. I'm sorry. I need to grow up."

"I imagine it's difficult seeing your little girl need someone other than you. You have nothing to be sorry for." He let her cry on his shoulder a little while longer, then gently reminded her the guests would be arriving shortly.

She nodded. The caterers were sticking close to the kitchen while she cried. She went to the bedroom to freshen up and put some make-up on while Steve let the caterers know they had free reign once again.

Embry and Marshall were the first to arrive. Willow's red swollen eyes alerted Embry to her father's arrival.

"I take it dad showed up."

Willow nodded.

"Did you send him away?"

Willow shook her head.

Embry looked to Steve for some verbal information.

Steve smiled slightly. "He'll be back at six."

Embry widened her eyes. "So, Mom, you're letting him come."

Willow swallowed the frog in her throat. "If it means that much to you, then yes." She dabbed her eyes. "I don't want to start crying again so let's just change the subject. Okay?"

Embry nodded. She fully empathized with her mother. She hated for anyone to see her cry too.

Willow bit her lip and went to the kitchen. "Do you need any help?"

She was shooed out of the kitchen so she checked the fire. Steve had already added another log. It was crackling just fine.

She turned from the fireplace and went in search of something to do, anything to do. This night was supposed to be perfect. Everyone she knew was coming to celebrate Embry's engagement. She needed to pull herself together. Why did I think he wouldn't come? Why didn't I prepare myself for the worst? She ducked into her bedroom to take a few deep breaths. Come on, Willow. You can do this. You're made of stronger stuff than this!

She had no idea why but lately she'd been more emotional. She was a straight shooter. A woman who saw the logic in things and pretty much called it as she saw it. The girls in college would cry over commercials and Willow wondered what was wrong with them. Now, it was her turn. Especially if the commercial had to do with kids growing up and leaving.

Willow decided to talk to her doctor. Maybe she was peri-menopausal. *There must be some reason I'm acting like this!*

The doorbell rang and she took a deep breath. *I shouldn't have any more time to be morose. My guests will keep me busy.*

As the evening spent, Willow found herself loosening up and laughing. Every time the doorbell rang, she would jump a little expecting Alex to be on the other side. Instead, it was always one of their other guests. She had to admit, she finally started to worry a little, especially when she caught sight of the frown lines on her daughter's face.

Guests were milling around, eating hors d'oevres, and chatting with the young couple about their wedding plans. Willow finally figured Alex wasn't coming. He'd disappointed her daughter once again. Perhaps she would learn her lesson. Willow learned long ago the man was not to be trusted. She was about to pull Embry aside when the doorbell rang.

Willow answered the door. Alex stood on the other side. He tried to straighten his windblown hair and make himself presentable before facing his grown daughter. Without thinking, Willow reached out to wipe some chocolate from the corner of his mouth.

He took a quick step backwards. "What are you doing?"

"You have a little something…" She pointed.

He touched the side of his face. "Here?"

She shook her head. "No, down, by the corner of your mouth."

His eyes lit up. "You can kiss it off. Nothing more intimate than a little chocolate kiss between lovers."

A deep voice behind her said, "Lovers?"

Alex swept by her, smiled, and shook Steve's hand. "Hi, I'm Alex. Willow's ex."

"I'm Steve. Willow's current."

Willow looked at both men. "Hello, I'm right here."

Alex turned back to her and lowered his voice to a loud whisper, making sure Steve heard every word. "No worries, I couldn't forget about you that easily."

Willow rolled her eyes and shook her head as she walked away, pointing toward Embry as she left. Steve stood a good six inches taller than Alex so he crossed his arms and stared the man down as he traipsed after Embry.

He watched the young woman hug her dad. The room wasn't large enough to hide from her excitement.

"You made it!" Embry giggled.

Steve groaned then went in search of Willow.

Chapter 2

She was waiting for an explanation to the possessive exchange he'd had with Alex when Willow heard Steve's phone buzz. "You gonna get that?" She nodded toward his pocket.

He frowned then pulled his phone out. "The station. I gotta take this. I'll be right back." He stepped outside so Willow's eyes searched the room for Embry and Marshall. She knew they'd be ignoring their guests and hanging out with Alex. *Get a grip, Willow. He just got here.* She chastised herself and started for her daughter's side.

Steve opened the door and motioned for her. She furrowed her brow in question but went to him. "What's up?"

He sighed. "I, uh…I have to take Alex in for questioning. Old man Thomas just found Alex's girlfriend dead in their shared room." He paused. "I don't want to upset Embry, not tonight. But…" He glanced Embry's way. Her face was radiating happiness.

"Oh, that is terrible. What happened? An accident?"

He shook his head. "I don't know. She was eating some chocolate and it appears she had some sort of reaction to it. It's probably a tragic accident. I doubt foul play is involved."

"That makes sense. Not even I knew he brought a girlfriend with him. He never said a word about her. So, I doubt anyone else did either." Her mouth opened slightly. "Unless, of course..."

Steve cut her off. "Your imagination is working over time. He gave her a concerned shrug. "Either way she's dead so I've got to look at all the possibilities—which includes talking to Alex." He looked to Embry again.

"Can you wait an hour or so? The party will be wrapping up by then anyway. Tomorrow's Valentine's Day and a few people have plans for after the party. I don't think it'll be too much longer." She pleaded with him. She'd love it if Alex was locked up and the key went missing, but the heartbreak she knew would be on her daughter's face kept her from encouraging Steve to take him now.

Steve watched the young woman interact with her father. "She's going to hate me if I don't wait. I'm going to keep a tight leash on him though. If he did have something to do with this,

I don't want him thinking he can slip away with no consequences."

Willow nodded, grateful that Embry's hopes for her dad wouldn't dissolve quite so quickly. At least she had the party to think good thoughts.

Steve planted himself on the chair nearest Alex and tried to look as though he wasn't listening to everything the man said. Embry, on the other hand, was hanging on his every word. Her face was positively glowing. Willow shook her head at both of them and wandered around the room, chatting with guests.

Marshall's parents were quietly talking in a corner and glancing every few seconds at Alex and Embry.

Willow approached them. "Hi, you two enjoying yourselves?"

Mrs. Yates quickly recovered from her whispered conversation with her husband. "Oh yes, it's a lovely party. The food is delicious. I must have that recipe for those meatballs. Whoever made them?"

Willow smiled. "I did. I had most of the food catered but Embry wanted a few of her favorites—the meatballs being one of them."

Mr. Yates popped one in his mouth and despite the glare from his wife, he mumbled,

"Delicious." At least that is what Willow thought he said. He shrugged at his wife and grinned at Willow.

Willow decided straight away that she liked Marshall's parents. They were good, down to earth people. "Do you have any plans for Valentine's Day?"

Mrs. Yates blushed.

Willow stuttered. "Oh, maybe I shouldn't…"

Mr. Yates cut her off. "Nonsense. I'm taking my blushing bride away for a couple of days of romancin'." He nodded toward the Chief. "How about you and Chief Grice?"

"Oh…well, he told me to keep tomorrow evening free. I guess we're doing something." She watched him watch her ex. "I, um, think we should open gifts, don't you?"

Willow closed the door behind the last guests then turned to Embry and Marshall. She hesitantly smiled.

"Mom, what's wrong?"

Willow had never been able to hide anything from Embry, no matter how hard she tried. She blew out a hard breath. "Let's sit down." She motioned for Embry, Marshall, and Alex to follow her and Steve to the dining table. She looked to Steve to take over the conversation.

Steve took his cue. "Alex, I'm sorry to have to tell you this, but your girlfriend passed away back at old man Thomas' place."

Alex stood abruptly. "What? That can't be right. Cub…I mean, Kelly, was fine when I left her."

Steve told him to sit back down. "Did you purchase some candy for her for Valentine's Day?"

"No, I'd never do such a thing. She's…I mean," He gulped. "She was diabetic."

"She died after eating a couple pieces of chocolate. I would like you to come down to the station with me and answer a few questions. You can probably help us the most with her personal information." He purposefully made Alex's trip to the station sound routine for Embry's sake. He did want to question him further, but Embry didn't need to know that.

Alex stood again and started pacing. "She wouldn't have eaten chocolate. She knows better. This doesn't make sense."

Steve rose from his chair. "I don't know what to tell you except she did eat from the box of chocolates. You can help us find out why."

The two men left without a word to Embry. Willow shut the front door behind them, let Clover out of the bedroom, then approached her daughter who was in Marshall's arms. "Sweetie, I'm sorry about all that."

Embry burst into tears all over again. "Mom, does Steve think Dad murdered his girlfriend?"

"Honey, most likely it's a horrible accident. I doubt anyone murdered her. Maybe she thought a piece or two of chocolate would be okay. I mean, your grandfather used to sneak food he wasn't supposed to eat all the time. Who knows, maybe she did the same."

Embry sniffled and left the comfort of Marshall's embrace. "You heard Dad. He said she knew better. She never ate sweets."

Willow shook her head. "I don't know what else to say. We'll know something here soon, okay? Try not to worry. I'm sure everything will be fine."

Embry allowed Willow to wrap her in a hug. "I hope you're right."

"Me too. Me too." Not for a million dollars would Willow admit not an hour earlier she wanted Alex locked up and the key thrown away.

Chapter 3

Clover sat with her head cocked as she watched Willow pace.

"Clover, nothing. He hasn't called. I don't know what is happening. I don't know what to tell Embry." She glanced at her watch. He should know something by now. She punched his number in her phone. "Voicemail, Clover."

She cocked her head the opposite direction then woofed.

Willow grabbed her keys and patted Clover goodbye. "Good idea. The police station it is."

She parked her jeep at an angle at the curb then booked it inside. "Where's the Chief?"

"Um, you can't go back…" He yelled toward her retreating backside.

She popped in the observation room to see Alex resting his head on his forearms. Steve wasn't around so she waited. The door opened and an anxious chief of police walked in and stood in front of her.

"What do you think you're doing?"

"Uh…uh…well, I've come to see what's going on." She was genuinely offended.

"Willow, you're too close this time. This man used to be your husband."

She scowled. "Briefly. Would it help if I said I wouldn't mind you locking him up and throwing away the key?"

"See? That's exactly what I'm talking about. You're too close! You can't be objective."

"Objective? Of course, I can. If she died of natural causes and he's innocent, I'll even let him come to the wedding. What do you know, I can be objective." She said with attitude.

He shook his head then put his hands on his hips, knowing full well if he didn't work side by side with her she'd do her own thing. "Okay, but you've got to promise me you won't do anything, anything at all without me with you. If there's anything to find out that is."

She stuck her hand out. "Deal."

He took it, knowing very well he may regret his decision. She didn't leave him many choices. Working with her was better than her going off half-cocked. "Deal."

Willow wasted no time. "What do you have so far?"

Let me send Alex on his way then I'll fill you in.

Willow watched on the other side of the glass as Steve gave Alex the normal "don't leave town" etc. etc. speech then waited somewhat patiently for him to return. Finally, the door opened.

"Let's go in my office." Steve led the way. "I didn't think he was ever going to leave. Most guys want out of here as fast as we let em' go." He pulled out a chair for her then sat behind his desk and opened a file. "We still haven't determined if foul play was involved. Apparently, Kelly, that's his—well, was his girlfriend, was diabetic. The chocolates were sugar free so that's not the issue and apparently, she was a stickler for following the rules. She always ate in accordance with her doctor given diet and never strayed. Alex was adamant she was conscientious about her health. She knew the consequences and never chanced it."

"Alex may have been a heel, but I can't see him purposely buying a diabetic sugary candy."

Steve looked up. "Oh, and he insists he didn't buy her the candy."

"Then where did it come from?"

Steve shook his head. "I don't know. We're tracking down where the delivery came from. We'll know more then."

Willow was confused. "So, who in the world knew she was here?"

Again, Steve shook his head. "That's the weird part. Alex said coming was a spur of the moment thing. They're on their way west and decided to swing in for the engagement party."

"Did old man Thomas recognize the person who delivered the package?"

"Yeah, it was Teddy Braxton, the kid who worked at the pizza place then started his own delivery service. It's quite the little business he's got going on. Innovative."

"Oh, I know him. He picks up to-go orders from the coffee shop."

"You get to-go orders? For coffee?"

She shrugged. "I guess people like our coffee." She hesitated. "He's even picked up deliveries for the police station."

"What?"

"Um, your coffee, well, let's say it leaves a lot to be desired."

"There's not a thing wrong with our coffee. Sheesh. My men are getting…" He wisely closed his mouth.

"They're getting what?"

"Never mind." He looked back at the file in front of him. "Kelly Thomas, 32 years old, Caucasian, born in Chicago, Illinois. Female, owns her own business as a UBER driver? Ever heard of that?" He looked to Willow who shrugged and pulled out her phone.

"Hey, you said her last name is Thomas, as in the same as old man Thomas?"

"Yeah. Purely coincidence. No relationship whatsoever."

"I didn't think you believed in coincidence?"

"Where'd you get an idea like that?"

"From you?"

"Well, in this case, with nearly a million people in the United States alone with the last name Thomas, I'd say coincidence is a fairly reasonable explanation."

"You already googled it, didn't you?"

"You bet I did." He grinned, exposing that sweet dimple.

Willow paused ever so slightly as her eyes got lost in his then she shook her head and grinned back. "Coincidence my bottom."

"Well, in this case it appears coincidence really is a factor. She's never set foot in Oklahoma before yesterday and she has no family here, present or past. Old man Thomas has lived here his entire life. He's been our Santa Claus for last 12 years alone. His name is Edward Thomas and the candy box clearly read, "Kelly Thomas, be mine." So, coincidence it is."

"Well, that takes us back to who sent it. Seems to me someone knew she was here."

He stood up. "I'm going to have a word with Teddy Braxton. You want to tag along?"

Willow glanced at her watch. "Yeah. I've got a while before I must relieve Janie. She's losing half our help today, tomorrow being Valentine's Day and all. All the teenagers have hot dates and wanted off to get manicures and pedicures. So much has changed. I remember painting my nails…" She looked up and found him grinning. "Oh, sorry. I got lost in the moment."

"I haven't forgotten about our date, have you?"

She shook her head, hoping against hope that nothing interfered with their date night. She glanced at her own misshapen fingernails then said, "I'm looking forward to it. Where are we going?"

He smiled. "You'll see."

She loved a good surprise.

She climbed in Steve's truck, after he opened the door for her, of course. Somehow that never grew old. "Where does Teddy Braxton live?"

Steve grinned. "I think I'm going to let you experience it without being told."

She scrunched her eyebrows together. "So many surprises today." She leaned back in the seat and closed her eyes. February weather in

Oklahoma behaved psychotically. One day it would be 70 degrees the next day they'd experience an ice storm. One never knew. The day happened to be sunny, breezy, and a lovely 62 degrees—the perfect winter day as far as Willow was concerned. She left the north for more than just an ice cream shop. Shoveling a foot of snow every other day wasn't her idea of a good time.

Steve drove about 15 minutes before he entered a small trailer park set back off the country road they'd been traveling down—in fact, small might be too big. Tiny more aptly described the little gathering of single wide trailers. He climbed out then opened Willow's door.

Willow's gaze traveled over the five trailers. An older woman was snapping green beans in a beat-up recliner outside one unit. Two little girls were playing in the dirt, their mismatched clothing amazingly matching the dust perfectly. Both were in desperate need of a bath. They seemed happy and well fed, despite their obvious lack of the finer things in life.

Sagging curtain rods and faded drapes hung from the windows and porches with cinder block legs invited a visitor to approach a weather bubbled front door.

The woman snapping green beans acknowledged the pair with eyes that belied her interest. Beneath the worn leather exterior and the casual nod, she watched with hawk eyes, taking note of every move Steve and Willow made. Her heavy-lidded oracles didn't miss a thing.

Steve passed the old woman by, but Willow stopped in front of her. She wiped a stray gray hair with the back of her arm and spoke through her bare gums. "Help ya wit sometin?"

"Hi, we're looking for Teddy. Have you seen him?"

The older woman stared at Willow, deciding whether Willow was trustworthy. "Who's askin?"

Willow extended her hand. "I'm Willow Crier, I own the ice cream shop in town. My grandfather left it to me in his will, perhaps you remember him…?" She didn't get to finish her sentence. The old woman's eyes lit up.

"Course, I remember him. Ice Cream Man is what my youngin's used to call em'. We couldn't afford no ice cream but he was always handin' a little on the sly anyway." Her expression became alarmed. "I waddunt after no charity."

"Oh, no ma'am, I'm certain you weren't. We're just here to ask Teddy about his delivery service. I may have some work for him at my shop—if he's interested." Willow knew the remark was a little bit of a stretch but if the woman produced Teddy, she would find some deliveries for him.

"Why'd ya bring the sheriff with ya if that's all you're wantin' em' fur?"

Willow blushed. "Sheriff Grice and I are dating." Now she really felt like a heel so she added. "We do want to ask him about a delivery he made, but he's not in trouble. Honest. We just want to ask him a few questions."

The woman narrowed her eyes. She may not be the most eloquently spoken, or look the most fashionable, but she wasn't stupid. "What'd he do?"

Steve knew the people who lived behind their pride better than most. "Ma'am" He dipped his chin. "I just need to know who hired Teddy to deliver some chocolates for Valentine's Day. That's all. He didn't do anything illegal. Sometimes when you own a business you might have answers to questions others are asking."

The woman nodded. "Abbi, you run along and get Teddy." She went back to snapping her beans while dust colored the air as the little girl's bare feet pounded the earth.

Willow watched in awe as the woman's hands moved at lightning speed. Her yellowed fingers—a pack of cigarettes in reach—seemed to have a mind of her own.

A young man no more than 20, with disheveled hair, and low-riding jeans appeared on the front porch of one of the trailers. "Chief, you lookin' for me?"

"Hey, Teddy. You made a delivery to Old Man Thomas' place for a Kelly Thomas. Do you know who sent it?"

Teddy stroked his chin. "Weird thing. When the order was made the sender didn't give his name. Then, this morning I got a receipt showing the sender's name. Which is strange. Almost as an afterthought. Why'd you wanna know?"

Willow asked, "Teddy, who was the sender?"

"Oh, yeah" He pulled out his phone. "A guy by the name of Alex Neville."

Chapter 4

"Alex Neville, you lied! Why should I be surprised?"

Alex slowly sat up. He'd been told not to leave town but since he'd not done anything wrong, he packed up and headed out. Where was the harm in that? The deputy who pulled him over arrested him and put him behind bars. Willow standing on the other side of the bars screaming at him wasn't helping his headache. "Will you quiet down? I was trying to get some rest." He ran his fingers through his hair. "You sure haven't changed any. Thought you might have calmed down some by now." He glanced around the old-fashioned accommodations. "You sure did pick a doozy place to live—the very definition of a hodunk town!"

Infuriated, she turned to Steve and threw her hands up. "I give up. Sentence him for life. I'll explain to Embry."

She finally had his attention. "Woah, I didn't do anything wrong. Well, maybe I was trying to leave town but that's because I have places I need to be. Had nothing to do with Kelly.

Her dying was unfortunate but I don't see how an accident should put me behind bars." He turned to Steve. "Is she always like this?"

His demeanor assumed Steve agreed with his assessment of Willow's behavior.

Willow's fist was through the bars so fast Alex didn't see it coming.

"Ow! Did you see that? She popped me in the eye. I want to press charges."

Steve gave her a dirty look. "See what? I wasn't looking. Did something happen?" He pulled Willow into his office. "What part of objective do you not understand?"

Willow stuttered. "But…did you hear him? He provoked me."

Steve tightened his jaw. "You cannot be a part of this investigation. No…"

Willow interrupted. "It won't happen again. I promise. I let him get the best of me but I won't do it again. I mean it, Steve. I won't."

He tossed his head back and laughed. "I think he might have a shiner. You throw a mean punch." He turned serious. "Remind me to never make you mad."

Willow rested her head in her hands then looked up.

Steve closed in and wiped the tears from her cheeks. "Hey, it's okay."

"No, it's not. You have a complete jerk locked up in your jail cell who happens to be Embry's dad. How is that okay?"

"Willow, we had no choice…"

"No, I know you didn't. He has deserved jail for as long as I've known him. He deserves whatever he has coming. It's Embry that I'm worried about. Not that idiot." She motioned with her thumb. "This is gonna kill her, Steve. Not only that, but he was leaving. Did he even plan on saying goodbye to her?"

"I thought you wanted Embry to know what her dad's really like?"

She pulled away and crossed her arms. "I do, but…" She paused, "…I don't. If that makes any sense at all." She sighed. "As a parent, as a mom, all I've ever wanted to do was protect her."

She looked up, her quivering lips indicating a good cry was coming.

Steve pulled her back to his arms and just held her. Sometimes there were no words. Especially when there were no answers.

The two stood there for a moment until a commotion beyond the closed door garnered their attention.

"That sounds like Embry." Willow opened the door to find her daughter madder than a wet hen.

"Embry, what are you doing here?"

"Dad called me. He's being held like some common criminal." She shot Steve a menacing look.

Steve raised his eyebrows but let Willow address her daughter. A little grace went a long way.

Willow refrained from a quick comeback. Instead, she took Embry by the arm into Steve's office. "Calm yourself down. How many times have I told you to get the facts before you react?"

Embry folded her arms and just stared at her mother.

"Your father was told not to leave town. His girlfriend is lying on a slab at the morgue. Do you want to know what he did? He was leaving town. One of the deputies caught him outside town, bags packed, headed down the highway. And do you know what his explanation was?" Willow crossed her own arms to make a point. "He said he had places to be."

Embry's face paled. "That's not what he told me. He told me Steve was jealous and had a personal vendetta against him. Steve decided Dad killed Kelly even though it was an accident." She turned her chin upward, just a little. "And only because you wanted to get back together with dad and he had to turn you down." Her chin went up even further.

Willow had never heard a more ridiculous story. "What? And you believed him? Surely I raised you with a little more common sense than that!"

Embry struggled with her desire to see her parents reunited, no matter how much the odds were against it. "It could happen."

"No, Embry, it cannot. I won't let it."

The corners of Embry's mouth turned downward. "You won't even give him a chance."

"You have no idea how many chances I gave your father. I could always give you a history lesson if that's what you're looking for. Or you could trust me, like you've done your entire life."

Embry turned and stomped out the door.

Standing before Alex, Willow wanted to slap the silly grin off his face. Instead, she turned to Steve. "Do you still have an electric chair in this place?" She turned back to her ex-husband and took pleasure in seeing Alex's grin disappear. "You do realize Oklahoma is a death penalty state, right? The consequence of committing a cold-blooded murder is death. We're a little too backwards in this here hodunk town for lethal injection, but we get by with the chair. It hasn't failed us yet. We might have to try a few times, but we get there eventually." She turned and stomped out of the jail, feeling a little better knowing the shocked look on his face wasn't going to leave any time soon.

Willow stood on the sidewalk. Her attention was pulled in so many different directions, each important, although nothing as important as finding her daughter. Steve's voice whispering behind her captured her attention first.

"Give her time. She needs to think this through. She'll come to the right decision. You raised her right."

She sighed. As much as she wanted to chase the girl down and talk some sense into her, she knew it would only make matters worse. She wasn't often at odds with her daughter. Part of her feared Embry would realize what a failure she'd been and want nothing to do with her. The other part of her knew Embry needed her as much as she needed her daughter. She nodded and turned into Steve for comfort.

He held her on the sidewalk, not caring who took notice. "Want to go to your shop for some coffee? You've got me spoiled. I may have to invest in a better machine for the office."

She murmured in agreement but didn't let go. She wasn't going to be the one to let go first, not this time.

Steve put a little space between them then kissed her before taking her hand and leading her to her coffee shop.

Chapter 5

The next morning, Willow was surprised when Steve ordered two cups of coffee to go. When she looked at him in surprise, he said, "We've got to go look over Kelly's things."

She nodded. "I guess I am a little distracted."

"It happens to the best of us. But, if we want to get on your daughter's good side again we need to figure out what happened, tragic accident or not."

His phone rang and Willow watched his face lighten a few shades. His tone was somber.

"That was the ME. Kelly was poisoned. He said the chocolates were injected with cyanide."

"Cyanide?"

"Yep. This was no accident. Kelly Thomas was murdered."

Willow's shoulders sagged. "It's not looking good for Embry's dad." She sighed. "Who else knew her?"

He opened the truck door for her. "I have no idea. But we're about to find out."

***

Old man Thomas, Ed to his friends, exited his barn sucking on a stogie, as Steve and Willow climbed out of the truck. The sound of dogs barking could be heard from a distance. He wiped his hands on his bib overalls then shook Steve's hand and said between clenched teeth. "Chief. I imagine you're here to collect Kelly's stuff? I'll show you in."

Willow started a coughing jag from the smoke.

Steve did his best to ignore her and asked, "Has anyone been in the room since she died?"

"Nope. We stayed out just like the deputy told us. Course, he did let Alex get his stuff but Alex has been sleeping in the other guest room till we get this straightened out. I'm guessing she wasn't checkin' her insulin like she was supposed to. I've got diabetes myself. Tricky business. Nothin' to let go."

"She didn't die due to diabetes. She died because she was poisoned." Steve watched Ed's face scrunch up. He genuinely looked surprised.

"Are you sayin' she was murdered?"

"That's what I'm saying. She was most certainly murdered. Your guest room has become a crime scene, in fact, your whole house has. I'm gonna need you to give us some space to look through everything. Deputy should be here any time with a warrant, not that I think you'll demand one. Just like to do things the right way, if you know what I mean."

Steve handed Willow a pair of plastic gloves which she dutifully put on. As soon as Deputy Tucker arrived, they entered the rather plain looking house and the subsequent plain looking guest room. Willow started searching Kelly's purse while Steve looked through the closet. Willow glanced at Kelly's identification and credit cards, being careful to put everything back where it originally was stored. She peeked at her pocket size address book. Nothing stood out. She searched every pocket but nothing turned up outside the normal. She whistled when she noticed the brand: Hermes. "Wow. I mean, wow."

Steve turned toward her. "What did you find?"

"Her purse."

He glanced at the grey bag. "It's a purse. Same as any other."

Her eyes widened. "This Hermes purse cost more than some people make in a year."

"You're kidding me, right?"

She shook her head. "I kid you not. They're crazy expensive." She held up the purse and the link she'd found on her phone. "Almost 60 grand for this thing."

Steve's mouth dropped. "You're not kidding."

"Not unless it's a knock off, but I don't believe it is."

"You seem to know a lot about purses."

"Not really. I do recognize the name, don't you?"

"Now that you mention it, yeah. I guess I do." He picked up the purse and swiped his hand over the leather. "Wonder where someone like Kelly would get the money to buy something like this."

"I have no idea. But, I think you should get your men on it. There's more to Kelly than bleached hair and implants."

When they'd finished searching everything, they found nothing. Nothing that would indicate anyone in Ed Thomas' house poisoned the woman. All three turned up a big fat nothing. Well, not quite nothing. There was the purse to consider. No ordinary woman had a Hermes bag. Kelly was not ordinary. Willow wondered what made her so special.

Steve led the way outside as a Volkswagen Beetle pulled in the driveway.

Willow started toward the garage and the sound of barking dogs while Steve waited for the woman to get out of the little car. Old man Thomas quickly exited the barn and tightly shut the oversized door. "Hey little lady. You should meet my gal. Her name's Betty Lou and that's her now." He expertly guided Willow away from the barn and back to the gussied-up woman standing next to the bright yellow car. Willow looked over her shoulder only to be redirected, again.

"Do you have a lot of dogs?"

"Oh goodness, no. I own a kennel. Folks give me the good pleasure of takin' care of their doggies while they go on vacation or whatnot. Keeps me from getting too lonely."

"Sounds like a lot of dogs in there. Some of them sound mean." Not one to beat around the bush, Willow asked, "How do you know Alex and Kelly?"

Willow never got her answer. Instead she heard, "…I'll give her a piece of my mind. Tell me where that floozy is," as she approached Steve and, who she assumed was, Ed Thomas' gal.

Ed waddled a little faster. "Betty Lou, honey, just calm down."

"I ain't calming down, Ed. That tart with her fake blond hair and her fake big ole' boobs is gonna get a piece of this." She held up her fist.

[43]

"And them skirts she was wearing! I could see all the way to Christmas!"

"She don't mean nothing, Chief. She's just a little hot headed." He whispered harshly to the woman who suddenly had the impulse to shut her mouth.

Steve looked from Ed to Betty Lou. "Do you want to tell me why you're so mad at Kelly Thomas?"

"Um…well, I didn't know she kicked the bucket. I don't like speakin' ill of the dead and all that." Her mouth said one thing, her expression said another.

"Betty Lou's been out of town. Her mama needed tendin'."

Steve decided to use the shock factor. "See, here's the thing. Anyone can send chocolates from anywhere in the world. You don't actually have to be in the same place to murder someone that way."

Betty Lou gasped. "You don't think…I mean, you can't think I had anything to do with it." She looked to Ed. "I didn't even know she was dead."

Ed shook his head trying to get her to shut up but Betty Lou wasn't paying any attention to him.

"I knew she was trouble when they got here last week. That's why I went off to see my mama."

Willow exclaimed, "Last week?"

Ed threw his head back. "Betty Lou, I told you to hush up."

She swatted him away. "She was walking around this place like she owned it. Battin' those long eyelashes at Ed so he'd take a shine to her. Everybody knew they was as fake as them watermelons under her shirt. Puh-lease!"

Steve turned to Ed. "Ed, why do I get the feeling you're not telling me something?"

"Chief, you're barkin' up the wrong tree! I swear on my mama's grave, I ain't hidin' nothin'. I swear. He came in a week ago but I got the feelin' he wanted to remain anonymous like. And well, I figure since I'm a real bizness and all, well, I should have those client attorney privileges."

"Ed, you're not an attorney."

"I know that. It's that sort of thing though. I don't have to say anything. My business is confidential." He grinned big. "Like a priest then."

Steve shook his head. "Trust me, you're no priest either. You two go nowhere, do you understand?" He started for the truck then turned back around. "You don't have a hidden stash of cyanide on the premises, do you?"

Ed shook his head. "No, I sure don't."

Willow was fuming as they climbed in his truck. "Last week? He's been here a week?" Her mouth dropped. "I wonder if Embry knew about this. I bet she did and she didn't say a word. I'm gonna…"

"Watch it. People have gotten into a lot of trouble when the wrong things come out of their mouth." He stole a sideways glance. "Especially in front of a police officer."

She nearly blew steam out of her nose. "A police officer? Is that what you think of our relationship?"

He realized his mistake as soon as it came out of his mouth. Talk about advice turning around to bite you in the butt! "Willow, I'm sorry…"

She already had her purse in her hands. "Stop the truck. Right now. Stop the truck."

"Willow, please. I'm sorry. I just didn't want you to say something or do something that might hurt you later."

She held her purse close to her and didn't say a word. She was logical enough to know she was being too sensitive, but her feelings were hurt enough she didn't trust herself to say another word. She scooted a little closer to the door and looked out the window. Now she knew without a doubt where her daughter came by her attitude.

Chapter 6

Willow groaned when she saw the young journalist waiting with a cup of coffee at one of the little tables by the front window. "Ugh. I forgot about him."

Thankful she was speaking to him again, Steve looked around. "Who?"

She nodded toward the young man. "He's a journalist doing an expose on small towns in America. How he chose Turtle, I have no idea, but I agreed to an interview. He called yesterday morning before the party. Free advertising, ya know?"

Steve had seen the young man around town with a camera hanging from his neck. "I've seen him taking pictures here and there and wondered what he was up to. That explains that."

Willow walked toward his table, saying, "I'll reschedule with him."

"Wait."

She turned around, waiting for Steve to explain.

"Do you find it odd he showed up about the same time as your ex? He's been here a week too. I didn't correlate the two before…when I thought Alex had only just gotten into town. Now…"

She tilted her head. "Coincidence?"

"Why don't you do the interview and find out? I'll make some phone calls and see if I can verify Betty Lou's story." He sniffed. "I think it's past my lunch time too. I'll see what kind of sandwiches Janie made today."

Willow could have told him the choices were fresh chicken salad and a caprese flat bread, but she stopped short. It took everything she had but she stuffed her anger down and tried to act like the mature responsible woman she was supposed to be.

She approached the young man and held out her hand. "I take it you're Murphy McCoy? I'm Willow. We spoke a few days ago."

He stood up and greeted her. "Nice to meet you. I just love your town. And your shop. The coffee is great."

She smiled and sat down opposite him. "Tell me again, which publication do you write for?"

He shuffled his notebook. "I work freelance. I…uh…pretty much sell articles as I write them."

"How many small towns have you already covered? Doesn't this get expensive without having a buyer already lined up?"

He seemed nervous. "This project is for a book I'm working on. I write other articles to sell individually...which is how I survive."

"Oh, okay. Which town were you in before this one?"

He paused, studying her a moment before he replied, "Jasper, Arkansas." He quickly moved the conversation forward. "Do you mind if I record our conversation?"

"No, I don't mind." She leaned forward to look at his notebook. He slid it out of view so she leaned back.

He asked a series of questions then took some pictures of her scooping ice cream with one of her snazzy aprons. She had several—handmade by a local woman. After the interview, she joined Steve at a table for two. Janie already had a cup of coffee waiting for her.

"Well, did you learn anything useful?"

She shook her head. "Nope, he seems to be what he says he is. He's traveling from one small town to the next looking for material for a book. He writes freelance articles then sells them to publications interested in his work. Him being here is just a coincidence, I guess."

Willow took a long sip of her coffee. She'd given up her white chocolate mochas due to the immense carb and sugar counts. She looked down and smiled just a tad when she noticed her thighs were just a smidgen farther away from the sides of the chair. Yes! It's working!

"What were you just thinking?"

Willow's head flew up. "What? Oh, nothing. Not a thing." She changed the subject. "Did you check Alex's phone records? Did he order the chocolates?"

Steve smirked. "Apparently, his phone was stolen. He said he hadn't noticed with everything going on. Until he tried to leave town, that is." He leaned back in his chair and sighed. "We're waiting on the phone company to fax his records to us. The guy can spin a good story, I'll give him that. And he's convincing. I'm guessing his charm is what attracted you in the first place."

Willow's thighs flew right out of her head. "What? Let me assure you, you have nothing to be jealous of."

"Jealous? Who said anything about being jealous?"

She just smiled. "What I can't figure out is, why would someone want to kill his girlfriend? I mean, who is she? Was someone following them? Did she…" Willow paled, "…or he do something somewhere else that got them into trouble? Will the killer go after Embry?"

"Woah, hold on just a sec. Don't be seeing trouble where there ain't any. This could have nothing to do with Alex and everything to do with Kelly. I might add, if someone wanted to kill Alex they could have. She was the target. It was her name on the chocolates.

She exhaled. "You're right. I'm probably getting worked up for nothing."

Janie came by with carrot cake cupcakes with cream cheese frosting. Steve immediately reached for one. Willow shook her head. "No, thank you." She took a deep whiff then turned her head. She refused to look at them. It's not free day!

Steve stopped midair with his cupcake then put it back on the plate. "I changed my mind. I really don't want one."

Willow laughed. "You're lying!"

He tried to keep a straight face. "I did change my mind. I shouldn't have said I didn't want one, but I really did change my mind." He addressed Janie. "Would you wrap one up to go?"

Janie laughed but nodded.

"You didn't have to do that. I'm a big girl, I can handle you eating sweets in front of me."

"I know. But, waiting will make our date that much better. Trust me."

She narrowed her eyes. "I'm intrigued. You gonna tell me what we're doing?"

"And ruin the surprise? No way."

Willow tried to keep the mood light, but, her mind drifted to her ex sitting in a jail cell and her daughter, who should be the happiest she's ever been, mad at her.

Steve reached across the table and took her hand. "I hope you're not worried about you and Embry."

She looked up, wondering how he'd come to know her so well in such a short amount of time. Afraid she'd turn into a blubbering idiot, again, she remained silent.

Steve started to go on then stopped when his deputy rushed through the coffee shop door. "Chief, you need to…ah…" He paused, looking from the police chief to Willow and back again. "We've had to take the prisoner to the hospital. He started sweating and was throwing up."

Steve stood up. "You could have called me."

Willow followed suit.

"Well, uh…you see," he looked sheepish and continued, "um…" He stared at Willow. "Ma'am, he said your dog bit him and he's really sick."

Willow shrieked, "What? He said what?" She turned to Steve. "I swear, Clover did not bite him. She growled. Her hair stood up on end, and as much as I wanted her to, she didn't bite him."

"Tucker, what exactly happened. Tell me what he said."

"Well, I was workin' at my desk and I heard him moanin' so I went and checked him out. He was sweatin' bullets and mumbling. I noticed some kind of nastiness on his hand so I rolled up his sleeve. His arm was runnin' puss and all red and swollen. That's when he said, a dog bit him and mentioned Willow's mean dog in the same sentence. His words were all mixed up, probably due to him havin' a fever and all. Doc said he's got himself a bad infection." He looked a little embarrassed. "Maybe even rabies."

Steve smiled at his new young assistant. "Deputy Tucker, here's the thing. He only just met Clover yesterday evening. There's no way a dog bite could have progressed that fast." He looked to Willow. "Just in case, is she up to date on her shots?"

"Of course, and she didn't bite him."

"I believe you. We just need to take precautions until we know what happened. Let's swing by your house and take Clover over to my sister's. She'll keep an eye on her and make sure she didn't get herself into any trouble running around your place."

"Is that completely necessary?"

"Willow, what if he came by your house when you were gone? What if he met up with Clover when you let her outside? You can't be 100% certain she didn't bite him. Let's take every precaution to keep Clover safe, okay?"

She crossed her arms. "Don't ask me to choose between my dog and that jerk. I can tell you right now who'll win that contest."

He shook his head. The woman was as stubborn as the day was long. Before he could answer he caught her backside as she disappeared through the kitchen door.

"Willow. Wait." He ran through the kitchen to the back door in time to hop in her passenger seat before she took off.

Chapter 7

"What happened to 'you'll do nothing without me'? Don't make me regret letting you help with this investigation." Steve paused slightly before adding, "If I have to, I'll lock you up to make sure you don't do anything that'll hurt you more in the long run."

She grunted. "You wouldn't dare."

"Try me."

Willow stilled briefly. "I wasn't going to leave without you."

He shook his head. "Willow, the wheels were rolling when I got in."

She rolled her eyes.

"Let's take care of Clover first. I called Beth and Garrett. They're expecting us."

Willow liked Steve's sister and brother-in-law a lot. In fact, she'd have a whole lot worse of an attitude if it was anyone but them Clover was going to be staying with.

She did a U-turn without answering.

Willow knew she was being childish but try as she might she couldn't let it go so she gave Steve the silent treatment the entire drive. Clover was going to spend the next couple of days cooped up away from her. Granted, at least Steve's sister was going to be caring for her, but, she'd be confused and lonely. Just the thought of that low-down scoundrel blaming her dog for something she clearly didn't do made her mad enough to pop him a second time. She could give him a matching set of black eyes.

She came to an abrupt halt and jumped out of her jeep. Her daughter wasn't speaking to her…her dog was being quarantined and the person responsible was in a hospital bed. Willow knew she was taking her anger out on Steve. The hurt and anger were too present to shelve them, try as she might.

Willow opened the front door to her loyal, loving dog and dropped before her. "You love me no matter what, don't you?" Willow hugged the large canine as if she were her only friend in the world.

Clover licked the salty tears from her master's face.

Willow sputtered, "You're going to go on a sleepover, okay?" As if the dog could understand. "I'll come and visit you, I promise." She sobbed, not stopping to spit out the dog slobber as the dog's tongue made contact with her open mouth.

Normally, Willow would have grossed out and used mouthwash.

After giving Willow a few minutes, he cleared his throat reminding her they needed to get moving. She complied by standing and gathering Clover's things. She loaded the dog and the bag of toys, food, dishes and dog bed into her Jeep. Clover called shotgun. Steve refused to play by the rules and put the dog in the back seat. Clover didn't mind. As long as she had a window she was happy.

Willow parked in front of Beth and Garrett's long outbuilding, the one that housed the kennel for some of the rescue dogs they took in. Until the vet was 100% sure Clover was fine, she'd be in quarantine. Of course, knowing Beth, Willow was certain she wouldn't lack for human interaction.

Beth came out to greet them and immediately enveloped Willow in a hug. "She'll be fine. I promise." Beth gave her brother a dirty look then led Willow and Clover into the building.

Steve looked to Garrett, who had joined them. "What did I do?"

Garrett shook his head. "Best to just go along with it. Half the time I have no idea what I'm apologizing for. I just know life is more peaceful when I do."

Steve cocked his head. "That's a little dark. I mean, is that how marriage works?"

Garrett sighed. "Sometimes." He paused. "When you love someone, sometimes you do things you wouldn't otherwise do. And Lord knows I love your sister." He followed the path his wife had taken a few minutes earlier then turned. "You coming?"

Steve shrugged and said, "Yeah, I'm coming."

Willow wiped her eyes, feeling better than she had all day. Sometimes a chat with a girlfriend made all the difference. Her eyes glistening with moisture, but bright with revelation, she offered Steve a smile as an apology.

Steve wasn't a dummy. He'd take what he could. He smiled back, letting her know all was forgiven. He watched her say goodbye to Clover then hug his sister. His sister whispered something in Willow's ear that was clearly meant for her ears only. The small group walked back to Willow's Jeep as a truck pulled up to the building.

Beth rolled her eyes. "That's the new Veterinarian, Doctor Drake. Doc McGee is on vacation and one of the horses is with foal. We normally don't use him but…" She shrugged her shoulders. "I think Old Man Thomas uses the new guy exclusively now for his kennel."

The young veterinarian joined the small circle. He was tall, excessively so, and his face was angular and expressionless. Willow instantly took a dislike to him. His eyes were shifty, looking about the place, almost like he was casing it.

Willow followed Beth as she led the veterinarian to the mare. Along the way, they passed Clover's stall. A low growl emitted from the dog's belly and the hair stuck up on the back of her neck. Clover was a very good judge of character. The vet was not someone who should be working with animals, probably not people either. Willow was sure of it. She murmured to the dog and petted her back. "It's okay, girl. He's not here for you."

The vet's eyes darted to the stall then quickly faced forward, falling in line behind Beth.

Willow peeked into the stall housing the pregnant mare. She was swollen and seemed irritable.

Beth waited for Doctor Drake to examine the horse. He walked around, felt her stomach, listened to her heart rate. Then pronounced her healthy.

Willow watched the interaction between the two. She didn't know a whole lot about animals, besides what she'd learned since acquiring Clover, but she could tell Beth was a little dismayed by the vet's proclamation.

"What about the vaginal discharge? Her udders are enlarged as well. Do you think she has Placentitis?"

"Oh, um, yeah. Let me check." He groped around the horse, trying to get a sample of the discharge. When he finally got a cotton swab in the general vicinity of the horse's undercarriage he determined she was ready to foal. "Looks like we're gonna have us a baby here soon."

This information caused Beth to panic. "What do you mean she's getting ready to foal. She has at least six weeks left. If not a little longer."

"I'm thinking your math is a little off. This mare is going to have her baby."

"I don't think so. Thanks for coming out. I'll wait for Doc McGee. He'll be back in a few days."

"Suit yourself. You'll be calling me though if she starts to deliver and needs help. I'll keep my cell on." He gathered up his supplies and showed himself out.

Beth rubbed the neck of her mare and the touch seemed to calm her. Willow heard Clover's bark and turned to see Doctor Drake standing outside her stall. He rotated enough to see they'd attracted attention so he turned and hurried out of the building.

"That guy's creepy." Willow couldn't help herself.

"He's a quack is what he is. He has no idea what he's doing. I couldn't stand the thought of him touching her." Beth visibly shuddered. "He gives me the heebie jeebies."

"He must be good with dogs. You said old man Thomas uses him for his kennel. Maybe he specialized in dogs. Aren't some vets small animal vets and some large?"

"Yeah, but you'd think he would have some general information—like a horse's baby is called a foal."

Willow shook her head. "Yeah, that is kind of strange." She petted Clover as she passed by. "I'll see you later, girl." The dog sat expectantly at the gate. The sight broke Willow's heart.

Chapter 8

Willow lowered her window as she and Steve rolled down the highway.

Steve said, "Enjoy today. Tomorrow the temperature is supposed to drop. The weatherman said we might get hit with an ice storm."

She turned to him. "Are we still going out tonight?"

He smiled.

"I thought after the way I acted you might have changed your mind."

He took her hand. "Yes and no. We still have a date and no, I haven't changed my mind." He paused. "Unless you have?"

"No. I'm really sorry for the way I was acting. I was taking my frustration and anger out on you and I was wrong."

"I'm new to this relationship stuff. If ever I do something that I shouldn't, and I'm sure there will be plenty of times I do, please just tell me. I promise I'm a quick study."

Willow's eyes lit up. "What should I wear?"

"Dress comfortably."

"You're still not going to tell me where we're going, are you?"

"Nope. You'll see."

Willow dropped Steve off at the coffee shop where his truck was still parked from earlier. Janie was tossing trash in the dumpster and stopped to chat with her boss and best friend as Steve pulled his truck from the parking lot.

"You seem to have calmed down. Everything okay now?"

"Still the same. Just a new perspective. I had a little chat with Beth, Steve's sister. I told myself long ago that I wasn't going to allow anyone but me to dictate my mood. Something she said reminded me of that. I was allowing everyone and everything happening around me to put me in a bad mood. I don't want anyone to have that kind of control over me."

"I like that. I'm gonna tuck that away and use it."

"Feel free. Everything covered for this evening?"

"Yep. You go home and get ready for your hot date. Any idea where you're going?"

"He still won't tell me."

"You wearing your new black dress?"

Willow shook her head. "He said casual."

"You've got to get that man to take you out all dolled up. Did you tell him you had to buy new clothes? The old ones were falling off?"

Willow sighed. "Maybe next time. For tonight, it's jeans and boots." She grinned. "But, I did get new jeans."

Janie laughed. "You had to. Did you box up your old clothes yet?"

Willow made a face. "I'm workin' on it."

"You're not going to gain it back. Give them away to someone who needs them." Janie tapped the hood with her hands. "You need to get on home so you can get ready. Casual doesn't mean grumpy."

Willow saluted. "Yes, Ma'am."

The quiet assaulted Willow as she walked through her front door. No paws on hard wood floors or swishing of the tail as Clover waited for her to acknowledge her. She could hardly believe this used to be normal, before she became a dog lover.

Willow wasn't a high maintenance kind of gal so getting ready didn't take very long. She finished blow-drying her hair then applied some make up. Her jeans were new, as was her sweater. February evenings could get fairly cool in Oklahoma. Even when the days were warm and sunny. She added some earrings and a bracelet to the ensemble, spritzed a little perfume, and thought she passed muster.

The knock on the door caught her attention.

Smiling, Steve said, "I'm glad you're okay. I've been knocking forever."

Willow shrugged. "My doorbell has flown the coop. Hopefully she'll be back soon."

He nodded, fully understanding. "You look lovely." He pulled her close. "You smell good too."

Willow pulled back. "You look…exactly as I left you."

He shrugged. "Good thing we're casual, right?" Steve led Willow to his truck. "Your chariot awaits." He held the door open for her then closed it behind and jogged around and got behind the driver's wheel. "I'm glad to see you wore jeans and boots."

"Are you finally going to tell me where we're going?"

"I'll tell you where we're going to start out. Will that be enough to satisfy your curiosity?"

"Maybe not, but tell me anyway."

He rolled his eyes. "We're going to start out with a visit to your favorite four-legged creature."

She smiled. "Clover. I miss her already. The house is so empty without her."

He grinned. "Let's go see her." He took off for his sister's house.

Willow couldn't help herself. "Does this date include food? Cause I'm starving."

"Have we ever had a date that didn't include food?"

She thought for a moment. "I guess not."

Willow was surprised to see Clover running around the ranch. "I thought she was in quarantine."

"Well, the reason I didn't have time to change is because I was working on freeing Clover. We had to run some preliminary blood tests and we'll have to wait for those to come back from the lab, but, it was pretty easy to see from the bite on Alex's arm, Clover was not the dog doing the biting. We measured the wound against a bite impression from Clover. They were not a match."

Willow threw herself at Steve and started crying. "Thank you."

"You're welcome. I hope you forgive me for taking her from you. I couldn't take any chances someone would misconstrue our relationship and think I compromised the investigation."

She just nodded as she jumped from the truck and called Clover to her.

Beth smiled as she approached. "Everything is set up. I'll get out of your way."

Willow asked, "Should we ask…"

"Nope."

"But…"

"No. I get you all to myself." He led her into the same building that Clover and the mare were residing in, although to the opposite end where there was a lovely apartment.

Willow gasped when she saw what Steve had arranged. An intimate table set up with a white table cloth glimmered in the dim candle lit room. He led her to the table and pulled her chair out for her then placed a napkin on her lap. Willow glanced about. Candles were lit in various spots, at varying levels. In the center of the table was a tray of hors d'oeuvres. A bottle of wine was chilling in a bucket of ice. A vase full of red roses decorated a sofa table. She tried to take it all in.

"Help yourself. Eat well because we have an activity planned before the entrée."

She sampled bits of smoked salmon, caviar, lobster toast, and stuffed mushrooms. "Steve, this is wonderful. Did your sister make all this?"

"No, she didn't. I didn't either, if that is what you're wondering." He popped a mushroom in his mouth. "I have a good friend who happens to own a restaurant. She helped me with all this."

"Who?"

He cocked his head. "Really?"

Her mouth dropped. "Molly?"

"You sound surprised."

"Well, I didn't know she could cook like this. I mean, she makes wonderful home cooked meals at the café, but she doesn't serve anything like this."

He grinned. "You mean I was actually able to surprise you? You had no idea?"

"None whatsoever. And I can't believe Molly hid it from me."

They finished up the first course then Steve led Willow to the opposite end of the building, near the mare who was ready to foal. Two horses were saddled and ready for them.

"Steve, I've never ridden a horse."

"Never?"

"Never."

"Well, you won't be able to say that any longer, now will you?" He showed her how to insert her left foot into the stirrup and use the horse's mane to pull herself up and throw her right leg over the saddle.

"Won't I hurt the horse? Pulling its hair like that?"

"No, I promise you won't."

She followed instructions and the next thing she knew, she was sitting in the saddle. She grinned. "I did it." Almost immediately she realized she was sitting on an animal that truly had her life…on its back. Her smile disappeared. "We're going to go slow, right?"

"Would you relax? You'll be fine. You're riding the calmest horse on the ranch. She's getting up in years and doesn't have much get up and go left. She is happy to plod along. We can barely get her to gallop when we want her to."

"Okay." She patted the horse's neck. "Nice horse."

Steve chuckled. "Her name is Daisy." He explained how the reins worked in accordance with her heels and the bit in the horse's mouth. Once she was fully up to speed on how to control the horse, he led her out and into the pasture through a patch of woods. "There's something I want you to see." The sun was starting to descend. Steve helped Willow off her horse. He pulled a blanket out of his saddlebag and placed it on the ground. "When the clouds hang low, like they are today, the sunset is phenomenal. There's nothing like it. No artist has ever been able to capture the real thing."

He sat behind her, letting her use him as a chair back. Together they watched the sun scatter rays through the clouds and across the sky. The intensity was constantly changing, creating pillows of fire as far as the eye could see. Slowly darkness began to intermingle with daylight.

Willow turned to Steve with tears in her eyes. "Such beauty."

He grazed her cheek with his fingertips. "From where I'm sitting, the sunset comes in second." He lowered his lips and gently kissed her.

Willow's insides were officially mush. Her chest rose and fell as she experienced the rush attraction brought.

Steve broke contact. "Willow, I love you."

Chapter 9

Willow wasn't sure she heard Steve right. Her ears were ringing from the wind and her face was starting to freeze. She was also pretty sure her nose was about to drip. Talk about timing. "What did you say?"

"I said, I love you." He handed her his handkerchief.

"Oh. I was hoping it was my imagination." She said as she wiped her nose.

"That I said, I love you?"

"No, no, that my nose was dripping."

"Oh." Steve fell silent then hopped up. "We need to get back. Dinner is waiting."

Willow reluctantly allowed herself to be pulled to her feet. Even in the cold she loved being with Steve. She managed to mount her horse without help, a huge achievement of which she was very proud.

They rode home in near silence. Steve helped her off her mount and handed the reins to his sister who graciously volunteered to care for the horses.

This time when they entered the back room there were two covered plates at each place setting, a basket of bread with a dish of butter, two wine glasses and two water glasses as well as various side dishes. Steve pulled her seat out and again placed the napkin on her lap. He then took the dome off the plate.

Willow feasted. She felt pampered and loved. After a melt in your mouth filet, there were chocolate covered strawberries and crème brûlée. Steve already knew her so well. Or did he have help? "This was phenomenal. Thank you." She leaned back in her chair. "As good as everything was, giving Clover back to me was the best gift I could have asked for." She sighed. "Now, if you could just get Embry to see reason all will be well."

"I'm afraid she's as mad, or madder, at me than she is at you. In her eyes, we're both attacking her dad."

Willow nodded. She admitted she was being as stubborn as her daughter. In other words, her daughter came by her gift of stubbornness naturally—from her mother.

Steve stood and turned on a hidden source of music. "May I have this dance?"

Willow's jaw dropped just a little before she clamped it shut. She stood and took his outstretched hand.

Several songs later, there was a light tap on the door. Willow pulled away, feeling as if she'd been caught at something she wasn't supposed to be doing.

Steve opened the door to find Beth, his sister, on other side. "Is Clover in here?"

He shook his head. "No, I thought she was with you."

"Didn't she go on the trail with you?"

"No."

Willow joined them at the door. "What's the matter?"

Beth looked a little shaken. "I can't find Clover. Maybe she went out looking for you two and got lost. She doesn't know this land like she knows yours." She paused. "I haven't seen her for hours. I really thought she went with you on your ride."

Willow's stomach felt as if she'd just been sucker punched. "She was here when we got here. Where could she have gone?"

Beth shook her head. "I really don't know. Doc McGee came home early from vacation and came to check on our mare." She nodded toward the back of the garage. "Let's take the four wheelers out and call for her." She turned to Willow. "You stay here in case she comes back.

Steve and I know the land and we'll be fine going out after dark."

Willow walked around the ranch yelling, "Clover, Clover" repeatedly. She paused next to a log to catch her breath when a familiar scent caught her attention. She started to cough. She recognized that smell—Ed Thomas' cigars. On the ground were several butts from the man's nasty habit. She ran to the house and took Beth's keys for her Cadillac.

Chapter 10

Willow pulled up to Old Man Thomas' place just as Doctor Drake, the new vet in town, was exiting his vehicle. "Where is Ed Thomas?"

"Uh…I don't know. I just got here. He called me and asked me to come out. Something about some young reporter sneaking around with a camera."

"That would be Murphy McCoy. He is doing a series of articles on small town America. He probably wanted to talk to Ed about his kennel." They both trudged to the house. Willow pounded on the door. No answer. Dogs were barking from within the barn so she hurried that way, the gangly veterinarian keeping pace with her. It was dark so Willow used the flashlight on her phone to light the path.

Doctor Drake flipped a switch and light flooded the dirty room. He called out, "Ed, you in here?"

The dogs in the back of the building were practically coming unglued. She flung open a door and gasped, "Call the police." She ran toward Ed who was lying on the concrete, dead. "Someone must have hit him on the head. Everything is covered in blood. I can't see what is what."

Doctor Drake pushed her aside. "I'm a doctor. Let me have a look. He may have just slipped and fell. You call the police."

Willow wanted to smack him. Instead, she tried dialing. "No signal. Ugh, I'll be right back." She ran outside holding her phone up in the air hitting re-dial and hoping for a signal. Finally, she heard a ring.

Steve answered, "Where are you?"

"I'm at Ed Thomas' place. Steve, he's dead."

"I'll be right there. Don't leave." She hung up and ran back in the building. Doctor Drake was still leaning over the body.

"He's dead alright."

She rolled her eyes. "I could have told you that." She noticed a bloody chain choker with spikes in it under the cabinet next to the body. Something horrible pet owners might use to control their dogs. Dogs were still barking in the background. She didn't want to leave Doctor Drake so she stuck to him instead of going to check the dogs. She could do that as soon as Steve arrived.

She heard the sirens. A minute later Steve came barreling through the door into the interior room where she found Ed's body. She looked at him with abject horror.

"Are you okay?"

Doctor Drake stood up. "Looks like he slipped and fell. Hit his head. Bled out. Pretty simple really."

Steve turned to him. "Since when have you become our medical examiner?"

"Well…" He stuttered. "I was just giving you my professional opinion."

"You're a veterinarian. And according to my sister, a bad one at that."

The vet harrumphed and stalked off. "Fine. Your M.E. will tell you the same thing I told you. If you need me, you know how to reach me."

"Hold on. I didn't say you could go anywhere."

The vet seemed impatient. "I have had a very long day. I told Ed that on the phone when he called. Seems that photographer running around town was here snooping around, not sure why Ed felt the need to tell me about it but he did. Maybe that is a clue to your investigation. Not sure why Ed needed me. Perhaps one of the dogs had the sniffles or something. He was going on and on about his dogs."

At the mention of dogs, Willow took off in search of the dogs she heard barking. She called over her shoulder, "I'm going to make sure they're all right."

The first room was a long corridor with rows of kennels. The dogs seemed to be okay. They had fresh water and food. Their cages were clean. All looked okay. She was about to head back to the supply room, where she found Ed, when she heard a high-pitched whine. She walked the length of the cages and the dogs were making noise but none of them were crying.

She tried a door at the end of the corridor. "Locked." The whining was louder. "There's got to be a key somewhere." She went back to Steve and the body. "Did you perhaps find a set of keys on him? There seems to be a dog behind a closed door. I have a feeling it could be Clover."

Steve dug in Ed's pockets and produced a set of keys. "See if one of these will work."

She took off at a trot to see if the dog behind the closed door was hers. The last key she tried finally unlocked the door. She flung the door open to find Clover, muzzled, and chained to the wall. She tore the muzzle off her and unhooked the chain. "Oh, my baby. What did he do to you?"

Steve startled her. "And why?"

Chapter 11

Willow's phone was beeping like crazy. She finally took the time to look at it. "Embry. 27 missed calls."

She quickly dialed her daughter's number.

"Mom. Steve called. He said Clover is missing."

"I found her. She's safe now."

"He also told me Clover didn't bite dad. That dad lied."

Willow quietly confirmed Steve's report. "Clover didn't bite your dad. I have no idea why he said she did."

"Why would he do that?"

"I don't know. You'll have to ask him."

"Mom, I'm sorry. I just wanted dad to be…a part of my life. I was so afraid I'd lose him again."

"Honey…," Willow swallowed hard. She wasn't sure what to say. "…can you come over later? I know it's getting late, but we really should talk."

"Yeah. I'd like that. I don't think I'd sleep otherwise."

"Me either. In fact, why don't you plan on spending the night. We could use some mother—daughter time."

"Okay. I just got off work. I'll run home then come over."

Willow put her phone in her back pocket.

Every available hand was at the Thomas place. Deputy Tucker called out. "Chief, you're gonna want to see this."

Willow's eyebrows perked up. "What is it?"

The deputy got a little snarky. "I said Chief."

Steve cleared his throat to let his young deputy know he was listening in.

"Um, this way." He held the door open for her.

In another locked room, there were three pit bulls, chained and muzzled. They had been in one heck of a fight. Willow started to approach but Steve pulled her back.

"They're hurt."

"They're fightin' dogs. It would appear Mr. Ed Thomas wasn't exactly the model citizen. And to think he's been our Santa Claus for the past few years." He shook his head then he held up a bag. "Look what I found. This makes sense now. It's a dog choke chain that is used to break skin if need be, to keep a dog under control. I found it under the shelf in the storage room—not too far from Ed's body." He handed the bag with the bloody choke collar off to his deputy. "Let's find out if the blood on that collar is Mr. Thomas'. The M.E. just took the body. We'll know shortly if he was choked with that thing." He turned back toward the dogs.

She just nodded her head. She knew he'd find it. And she hadn't wanted Mr. know-it-all Veterinarian to contaminate the evidence. Clover was still trying to get Willow to hold her. Poor dog was traumatized.

Steve started to walk toward the door. "We'll let animal control know they have one heck of a job here to deal with."

The door flew open and Beth stomped in. "What did that man do to these poor dogs?" She headed straight for them. When Steve tried to stop her she ignored him, knelt, and began slowly introducing herself to one dog at a time. She whispered too softly for Willow to hear what she was saying. The dogs stopped growling and settled down quietly.

Beth said a little louder, so everyone could hear. "Doc McGee is on his way."

All three turned toward Doctor Blake as he said, "Why did you call him? I'm right here."

All three dogs jerked their heads in his direction and snarled. Beth waved him away and started whispering again.

Willow followed Steve, who had followed Dr. Blake, out the door. "What is she, the dog whisperer?"

"Pretty much. She started bringing strays home when she could barely walk herself. We've had everything from baby birds, to snakes, to litters of coyotes because of that woman. She loves all animals but dogs have to be her favorite. I've never met a dog she can't tame."

"Your sister is pretty cool."

"That she is."

Steve turned to Doctor Blake. "You're free to go. If you remember anything else, just give me a call. You never know what might be a turning point in the case. Something insignificant to you might make all the difference to me."

Doctor Blake nodded then walked away, still offended he wasn't asked to deal with the dogs.

They watched him as he climbed in his pickup truck. "He says Ed called him. Wasn't sure why."

That's what he told me too. He was just getting out of his truck when I pulled up. We got here within a minute or so of each other."

[82]

"Hmm…I guess we need to find us a photographer."

Chapter 12

All Willow wanted to do was fall into bed. She was exhausted. As they approached her house, she remembered Embry was there waiting for her. She rested her head against the back rest and sighed.

Steve patted her knee. "Everything is going to be okay." He parked in her driveway then walked her to the front door.

She leaned into him. "Thank you for a wonderful dinner. And for clearing Clover." The dog was running around the yard like she'd just been hyped up on sugar.

"You're welcome." He gently kissed her. "Straighten things out with Embry. Get some rest. Everything else will keep. I'll call you tomorrow."

"Yes, Doctor."

He smiled then walked back to his truck.

Willow smelled chocolate. "Embry, I'm home."

Her daughter walked out of her room with a towel on her head. "Hope you don't mind, I took a shower. One of the guests spilled his drink all over me. I smelled like a brewery."

Willow rushed to Embry and threw her arms around her. "I've missed you."

"I've missed you too. I'm sorry, Mom."

"It's okay." She pulled back and looked at her daughter. "It's not easy growing up without a dad. I guess I've never looked at it from your perspective. If I had, maybe I would have been more understanding."

Embry wiped the tears from her cheeks. "I do want a dad. But I don't want a jerk for a dad. Why can't he be normal?"

"Oh honey, I wish I had answers for you. For some reason, your father is only concerned about himself. When you become a mom or dad, your child becomes the most important person in your life. They are helpless and in need of you in every single way. Most parents get that. Some never do. I hate to say it but I think your father is in the latter group."

All was forgiven. Both ladies curled up on the sofa with a plate of brownies. "You know me too well. Speaking of knowing me, did you fill Steve in on my favorite foods?" She took a big bite of the luscious chocolate treat.

Embry mumbled. "I might have given him a heads up on a few things." She smiled, brownie crumbles stuck between her lips.

Willow grinned. "You did good." She took a drink of her hot tea. "When are you and Marshall celebrating?"

"Monday night." She swallowed more brownie. " I have the night off. Last night and tonight was crazy busy at the restaurant. There's no way I could have gotten off." She took another brownie. Both sat in a comfortable silence, enjoying their time together.

"Mom?"

"Yeah?"

"If dad's such a bad guy, why did you marry him?" Willow stared at the flames dancing in the fireplace. "I don't know."

"There must have been something that attracted you to him. Was it his good looks?"

Willow laughed. "Believe it or not, your father wasn't that good looking when he was younger. Some men age better than others."

"Then what was it?"

After a moment of recollecting, Willow answered. "I was a rescuer. Your father was a lost soul. He was reckless and alone and I was looking to do anything my parents said not to do. We got married after knowing each other exactly a month." She shrugged her shoulders.

"Do you regret it?"

"Nope. Cause I got you."

Embry snuggled into her mom. "Can I sleep with you tonight?"

"You betcha."

Murphy McCoy tried to make a hasty exit when he saw the police chief striding toward him with purpose. Unfortunately, the chief's girlfriend was also walking toward him and unless he wanted to plow her down, he'd better stay put. He raised his hands, accepting defeat. "Okay. You caught me. But I can explain."

Chief Grice raised his eyebrows at Willow. "This I have to hear, explain away." Steve pulled a chair out for Willow then sat down across from her. "I'm not exactly sure how one explains murder, but I'd love to hear it."

Murphy dropped to his chair. "Murder? What are you talking about?"

Molly approached their table then backed away when she heard the word, murder.

Steve waved her down. She grimaced then proceeded to take their order.

"I think we could use a couple cups of coffee. It's been a long night."

Molly's diner opened early—really early. So did Willow's coffee shop. She'd hoped they'd find the photographer at Willow's because the coffee was better. No such luck. He was perched at a table at Molly's Café, sucking down coffee and typing like a mad man.

Willow took a gulp of the bitter black liquid. "Molly, you could do something about this coffee."

"What, and compete with you?" She tapped the air with her hand. "Nah, my customers have come to expect this strong brew. If I changed they'd be disappointed." She filled up Murphy's cup. "Besides, it'll make hair grow on your chest." She winked at Willow.

Murphy was still stuttering over the murder comment.

Steve, an early riser and a natural morning person, spoke up. "Were you hanging out at Ed Thomas' place last night?"

"Well, yeah, but what does that have to do with murder?"

"He was found dead in the office of his barn. Right after the local vet got a call from him telling him you were creeping about the place. Why would he say that?"

Murphy's shoulder's drooped. "Look, yeah, I was out there. But I didn't even see Ed Thomas. He wouldn't answer the door. I tried to look around the barn but it was locked up tight, so I left."

"Why would you do that."

"Might as well tell you now. This whole operation is going downhill fast. I'm a reporter, just like I told you. But, I'm not doing a series of articles on small towns. Well…I am, but not as I led you to believe. I'm doing some investigative reporting. I'm following a dog fight ring, trying to nail them. If you don't believe me, I've got pictures to prove it. I really was in Arkansas before this. I'm trying to get as much proof as I can before I submit everything to the authorities."

He brought up a file on his computer and turned the screen so Steve and Willow could see.

Willow's throat felt dry. "Steve, do you see what I see?"

Several pictures on Murphy's computer caught Alex and his girlfriend, Kelly Thomas.

"I see it. Alex has a lot of explaining to do." Steve asked Murphy, "Did you take any pictures here? My guess is Ed Thomas was up to his elbows in dog fighting. I want to know who else was involved."

Murphy shook his head. "I've tried. Everything has been on hold since that girl died. Everyone was afraid there'd be too many police poking their noses around. So, they wanted to hold off until everything died down. Now, with Ed's death, I doubt I'll get anywhere near the ring here." He picked up his camera. "They thought I was there to take pictures and help promote the dogs for sale and stud services." He looked up. "The girl who died, she was a bigtime breeder. Made the big money, if you know what I mean."

Steve was incredulous. "And you didn't think to tell us this?"

"She ate some chocolate. I heard it sent her blood sugar sky high and killed her. I thought it was an accident. No sense in ruining my cover for an accident. Besides, what she did to those dogs—she deserved to die."

Steve raised his eyebrows. "Did you put her out of her misery?"

"Me? No. No! I'm a pacifist. I won't kill a fly. Of course, flies are innocent while people can be…" He stopped talking. "I'm not helping my cause, am I?"

Steve shook his head then signaled Molly for more coffee. "Do you have any cinnamon rolls left? My stomach is growling."

Willow held up two fingers. Molly nodded then held up three and waited for her response.

Steve watched as the two women used hand signals. "Is there a reason you two aren't speaking?"

Willow shrugged. "I felt guilty for ordering a cinnamon roll and using a hand signal was making me feel less guilty?"

"Oh, for Pete's sake, bring three. I'm sure Murphy could use some breakfast too."

Molly whispered, "So, Murphy didn't commit murder?"

Steve narrowed his eyes. "I'm not sure yet."

Chapter 13

Murphy was told he was a person of interest and not to go anywhere before Steve told him he could leave. He grimaced, just a little, when Steve took his laptop and camera into evidence. He didn't like to be separated from his equipment. Understandable but the only other option was Murphy going with the equipment. Apparently, he liked that idea even less than being separated from it.

Willow stood up. "Are you ready?"

"Ready?" Steve took a bite of his omelet. The cinnamon roll was just a breakfast appetizer. Willow had no idea there were breakfast appetizers.

"Yeah, we're going to confront Alex, right?"

"Can I eat first?"

She sighed then sat back down, her own stomach rumbling in the process. Molly stopped by the table and placed a plate of food in front of her. "It was just a matter of time."

Willow's eyes lit up. "I never thanked you for dinner. You did an amazing job."

Molly smiled. "Thank you and you're welcome. It was fun. I don't often get to make meals like that. My customers want home cooking for their day to day eating." She nodded toward the plate of eggs, biscuits and gravy. "Like this. Now, eat up. Solving murders requires energy."

Willow groaned. Between the engagement party, Valentine's Dinner, and now, chasing a murderer, she'd gone off her eating plan. She felt a cleanse in her near future. She took a bite and sighed, "This is heaven." She looked at Steve. "By the way, what happened to the ice storm?"

"It's coming."

"Sure, it is."

"Are you prepared? Do you have extra wood cut? Bottled water? Canned food? Propane for the grill?"

Steve sighed. "You'll see."

"Are you forgetting? I'm from the north. We have snow and ice pretty much all winter long."

"How long do you think you can go without power in the cold?"

She smacked her leg and laughed. "You call this cold? I gave away my winter coat to one of the homeless people on the street corner."

"Never mind."

Willow wiped her mouth. Both their plates were void of any food. "Can we go now?"

Steve tossed some cash on the table. "Yeah, let's go see what Alex has to say for himself."

As they drove, they discussed the case. Willow asked, "Do you think the murders are connected?"

Steve nodded. "They have to be. Two murders. One house. Both involved in dog fighting. How can they not be?"

Willow nodded. "But who did it? I mean, at first, I thought Ed's girlfriend, Betty Lou, was the culprit. Her jealousy over Kelly Thomas oozed with anger. But why would she kill Ed?"

"I thought Alex killed her. I just wasn't sure of a motive. There's no way he could have killed Ed. He has been shackled to his hospital bed for the past 24 hours."

Willow thought about it. "Do you think there could be two different killers? With two separate motives? Both motives involve dog fighting, but different?"

"I just don't know. Let's talk to Alex and see what he has to say." Steve parked in the special parking spot for police officers. He led Willow to Alex's room.

Willow pushed through the doors saying, "You lying piece of…" She stopped short. The bed was empty. And bare. In fact, the room was being cleaned.

Steve asked the gal working, "Where did the guy in this bed go to?"

She shrugged. "I'm just the cleaning lady. I don't know anything about the patients."

Willow followed Steve to the nurses' station. "I'm looking for Alex Neville. He was in room 322."

The nurse raised her eyebrows. "And you are?"

He held up his badge. "Turtle police Chief Steve Grimes."

"Oh. He was discharged by his doctor."

"He is supposed to be in police custody. Did he go with one of the deputies?"

"No, the deputy on duty by his door was called away on an emergency. His doctor took full responsibility for him. We learn not to question doctor's orders. Not if we want to keep our jobs." She gave the nurse next to her a little sneer.

Steve was getting irritated. "Okay then, who is his doctor?"

She shrugged. "I don't know. I've never seen him before."

Steve rolled his eyes. "Is there paperwork I can see?"

She tossed a file at him.

Steve glared at her. "Do you have a problem?"

The woman pushed her glasses back up her nose. "I think it's terrible what you're doing to the poor man. Just because you're…" she reduced her voice to a whisper and looked around. "…dating his ex-wife..." She looked down then muttered. "I heard she wasn't even a good wife."

Willow's mouth dropped then shut again. "What? I'll have you know I was a good wife. A really good wife. He was a…he was…nothing but a sperm donor."

The nurse addressed Steve. "So, it's true. You're doing everything to remind the poor man of the abuse he suffered at this woman's hand. Parading her in front of him like that. I'd think a police chief would be a little more professional." She turned to Willow. "You should be ashamed of yourself. Using your blackbelt on him like he was a sack of potatoes. Poor man says you sicced your dog on him. Some people never outgrow their meanness." She turned her back on the two and said over her shoulder as she walked away. "When you're finished with the file, just put it on the counter. Too bad I have to show you anything."

Willow's face was getting redder with each word out of the nurse's mouth. "If that dog bite doesn't kill him I'm going to. Just wait until I find him."

Steve replied, "You're going to have to find him first because if you don't, I'm going to."

Chapter 14

Steve took a few pictures of the doctor's release. Of course, trying to read a doctor's signature was difficult enough without having the help of a nurse. Sitting at his desk, he was waiting for Deputy Tucker to arrive to explain himself, and perhaps shed some light on what happened.

Willow was pacing. She'd already called Embry who promised to call if she heard anything at all from her father. Willow was doubtful he would call her. He had to know by now that Embry had come to her senses. He, as usual, would only be concerned with himself.

The door flew open. Steve and Willow both stopped, fully expecting to see Tucker in some state of dishevel. Instead, a tiny woman, maybe a whole 5 feet, runs through the door. Where is Kelly Thomas. I need to see Kelly Thomas."

Steve approached the young woman. "I'm sorry, Miss. Who are you?"

She was still upset. "I just need to see Kelly Thomas. Identify the body. Please. My name is Jennifer Thomas. I'm his niece." Now the woman was nearly inconsolable so Steve led her to the morgue, well, more like an oversized meat locker. She was sobbing, using her sleeve as a tissue. He felt sorry for her. She was obviously confused.

Steve found Kelly Thomas' storage chamber and pulled the body out. He uncovered her face and the woman screamed and fainted.

Steve caught the woman before she hit the floor. "It must have been too much for her. Seeing her aunt like this."

Willow was wetting some paper towels to wipe her face. "She did say she was "his niece." Willow's face paled and she whispered, "No, it couldn't be."

Steve was intrigued. He never knew which way Willow's brain was going to turn. "What?"

"You don't think this…this she is really a he, do you?"

He laughed. "I'm thinking the M.E. would have noticed if she was really a he."

"No. It's a thing. Haven't you read about it? People are having surgery because they don't think they were born right." She shrugged. "Or something like that. It's all over Facebook."

"I'm not on Facebook. Or Twitter. I don't watch television. And I don't read the gossip magazines either." Steve looked at her like she was insane. He'd heard a few rumors but he'd dismissed them as ludicrous. "She couldn't be...could she?"

They both looked at each other, Kelly Thomas, then lifted up the sheet. Both exclaimed. "No way!"

Willow felt her face heat up. "No, she's definitely a woman."

Steve turned away, his own face competing with Willow's. "Yep, she's a woman." He looked at the young lady resting on the chair. She was beginning to flutter. "No, she's got to be confused. I wonder how she heard about her aunt's death? I thought Kelly Thomas didn't have any living relatives. This case is getting more confusing by the minute."

The woman groaned and tried to stand.

Steve approached her. "Oops, you better stay seated. You've had quite the shock. Identifying a loved one can be very difficult."

Willow handed her the wet paper towel she'd been holding. "Maybe this will help."

"Who...who..." She pointed to the body still protruding from the locker. "My uncle..."

Willow took the woman's hand. "Did your uncle have surgery? Is that what happened?" She looked to Steve. "This is probably why we couldn't find any relatives." She turned back to Miss

Thomas. "I'm so sorry you had to find out like this."

The woman gasped and passed out again.

"Poor woman. I imagine it's quite the shock. Well, she is a he, and of course, there's the issue of being dead. Just one would do me in. Both, I'd pass out too."

Steve shook his head and pressed some cool paper towels to the woman's face. "Miss Thomas. Miss Thomas."

She groaned a few times and blinked. "I'm sorry. I haven't eaten a thing. And all this…" She waved her hand in the direction of the corpse. "…has been a little too much."

Steve handed her a bottle of water. "Maybe this will help."

She took a long drink then said, "I think there's some sort of misunderstanding. I received a call today letting me know my uncle was killed at his ranch. Kelly Thomas is his name. Or I guess, it was." She shrugged.

Steve asked, "Do you mean Ed Thomas?"

"Well, Edward is his middle name. Everyone in the family calls him Kelly though. I just thought he would be called by his first name here at the morgue."

Steve turned to look at Willow then found the paperwork on Ed Thomas. "You're right. His first name is Kelly. Spelled Kelley." He put the paperwork down then pulled out the correct body. "I'm so sorry for confusing you. The gal we showed you, her name is Kelly Thomas. We thought it was quite the coincidence your uncle and this lady shared the last name. The fact they share the same first name...well, that opens a whole new list of questions."

Ed Thomas' niece identified the body then asked about his property. "Do you think it's alright if I stay at his place? I'm kind of short on cash."

Chapter 15

Deputy Tucker arrived in a flurry of apologies. "I'm sorry, Chief. I got a phone call from my girlfriend's brother. He said she'd been in an accident. But, when I got there, there wasn't any accident. I tried calling her and her phone went right to voicemail. Turns out, she wasn't in an accident at all. But, her phone was stolen."

Steve muttered, "What is up with all the stolen phones. Do we have a phone thief in Turtle? Alex's phone, now your girlfriends." He sighed. "What happened to staying with the prisoner? He's missing."

"I handcuffed him to the bed. I thought that'd keep him in place." He ran a hand through his tousled red hair. "I'm real sorry."

Steve waved him away instructing him to file his report.

"You know what this means, right?"

Willow said, "I believe so. Kelly's death may have been unintended. Ed may have been the intended target all along."

"The only thing I don't get is, why use his legal first name on the candy? If the killer meant to kill Ed, then why not just have the candy sent to Ed Thomas. That would have been a lot easier and he definitely would have eaten the candy. The poison would have done its job and Ed would be dead instead of Kelly, well, he's still dead but sooner. I guess." She grimaced. "And perhaps Kelly would still be alive. And maybe Alex would never have been put in jail and Embry wouldn't have gotten mad at me…and Clover wouldn't have been dognapped. That's a lot of what ifs!"

Steve shook his head. "You've confused me. That's okay. We've got to move on. We need to figure out if Ed was the intended target or if both Kelly and Ed were targets and we need to know if they were both killed by the same person. There is a lot riding on us finding Alex. He knows the answers to this mess, I'm sure." He filled his coffee cup then took a drink. "Yuck. I've got to get a new machine." He dumped the thick black liquid down the sink. "Feel like grabbing a cup of coffee? I'd like to run out to Ed's place and see how his girlfriend and niece are getting along. Perhaps we'll learn something new.

Willow managed to lasso her wandering mind to pay attention. "Like how Betty Lou was his partner in the dog fighting business and his niece killed him to inherit the ranch?"

He cocked his head. "How did you come up with that?"

"Isn't there some kind of rule about most murders being committed because of love or money? Seems to me you've got both."

"You're making a big jump from girlfriend to partner to murder. And we have no idea if his niece inherits a thing. She may be a grieving niece, nothing more."

"Hmmm…we'll see about that." Willow marched out to the truck needing coffee as bad as Steve. "Where in the world can Alex have gotten off to? Too bad that nurse was being difficult. I'm tempted to go back and give her a piece of my mind!"

The part timers at the coffee shop quickly filled their coffee order and the two of them were on their way back to Ed Thomas' ranch. "Did Betty Lou say she lived there?" Willow wondered.

"I believe she does. In her statement, she listed Ed's address as her home address." He paused. "I didn't think about that before I gave his niece permission to stay there. Wonder if the two women will get along?"

Willow took a swallow of her coffee then grinned. "We're about to find out."

As Steve stepped outside the truck he took a long look at the sky. "Storms almost here. You sure you've got everything ready at home?"

Willow answered, "I'm a northerner. We don't get ready for ice storms." He was worrying for nothing. If she'd stayed home every time there was ice or snow on the roads when she lived in the northern states, she would never have gone anywhere in the winter. Besides, the Jeep was four-wheel drive, she had firewood and a grill. What else could she possibly need?

The entire front lawn at Ed's place was covered in clothing. Willow picked up a pair of sexy underwear and a pair of granny panties. She shrugged. Call her old fashioned but she'd much rather have a pair of underwear that didn't consist of a string in her butt. How uncomfortable would that be? She wouldn't want to know! "Looks like you should have rethought the "niece staying at the uncle's place" idea. I'd say we have two alpha females going at it." The screaming from inside the house confirmed the clothes on the lawn weren't a case of laundry gone wild.

Steve marched toward the front door.

Willow yelled after him. "I'd be careful if I…"

A fry pan flew out the door and hit him upside the head. Steve dropped like a fly gone to meet Jesus. Willow rushed to his side. He was down and out for the count. The bump on his head was going to give him a horrid headache later. He groaned a little then dropped back off. She glanced at the cast iron skillet, groaned and said, "Mary Tucker's famous skillet apple cobbler. Someone is going to pay!"

Willow opened the door and walked in the kitchen only to find herself in the middle of a food fight. She was hit with lemon meringue pie on one side and a bag of flour on the other. She took a swipe of the pie with her tongue. "Mmm…" She felt something hit the side of her head and ooze down her face. The two ladies continued to whip food at one another as if Willow wasn't there. She tried to get them to stop but they wouldn't listen. For once in her life she wished the southern ladies of Turtle didn't cook so good. Want to eat well? Have someone in the family die. Every woman between the ages of 23 and 98 showed up with their own specialty—from pineapple upside down cake to pigs in a blanket to boysenberry jam—for the grieving family to partake (and hopefully brag about) in.

Willow ice skated across the floor in an attempt to get Betty Lou to see reason. "You're messing up your lovely kitchen. And you're wasting all this food." She yelled but couldn't be heard above the profanities being hurled across the room. Before she knew it, Willow had a handful of what seemed to be tatertot casserole and threw it at Jennifer Thomas. She had officially joined the food fight.

Jennifer yelled, "Hey, that was gonna be my supper. Why I oughta…" She approached Willow with a bowl of pink fluffy stuff and turned it upside down on Willow's head. "This isn't your fight."

Willow heard a voice clear behind her and she turned around in time to see chocolate pudding drip down Steve's face. She froze. As did the other two women.

"What in the world is going on in here?"

That was all it took. All three women started speaking at the same time.

Jennifer Thomas said, "This aging drama queen thinks this house, and everything in it…"

Betty Lou said, "She thinks she's gonna waltz in here and tell me what…"

Willow said, "I was just trying to stop them so no one else got hurt and they…"

Steve whistled—a loud piercing sound Willow had only heard about…never actually experienced.

All three clamped their mouths shut.

Steve wiped chocolate goo from his eye before continuing. "I don't want to hear another word—from anyone—until you're cleaned up and ready to speak like grown adults. Now, get yourselves cleaned up. Now."

Chapter 16

All three women were lined up on the couch. Willow in the middle feeling extremely out of place. Both Jennifer and Betty Lou were freshly showered and in clean clothes, despite the enormous amount of clothing on the front lawn. Willow, however, found an oversize t-shirt and a pair of sweatpants from the newly deceased's closet. She still had copious amounts of food in her hair. There's only so much a comb can do.

Steve was seated across from them on the only decent chair available. One of the ladies, or both for all Steve knew, had slashed cushions making them virtually useless. The only reason the chair he was using was still in one piece was it was solid wood. Neither of them had ventured to the barn for a sledge hammer. He guessed that could still happen—if he turned his back. "Now, one at a time. Tell me what is going on." He glared at all three of them, but especially at Willow.

She opened her mouth then clamped it tight and ever so slightly tilted her chin up. Why does this man infuriate me so?

Betty Lou didn't resist in the slightest. "This…this faker came right in my house and told me to get out…of my own house. Says she's Ed's niece and his heir. Says this is her place now. Can you believe the nerve?" She wiped an imaginary tear from her eye. "My sweetheart ain't even in the ground yet. She's already trying to lay claim to his stuff." She huffed a little more and tried to conjure up a tear. "Some people. Ain't got a classy bone in their bodies."

"He's the one who said this place was mine." Jennifer pointed to Steve.

"Woah, hold on a minute. I never said such a thing."

"You did too. When you were showing me the body. You said I could stay here."

"I said you could stay here…temporarily. I did not say this place was yours. Ed's lawyer will let us know who this place belongs to."

Betty Lou erupted. "We've been together for so long, we're common law married. I'm sure of it. I don't care what no lawyer has to say. I'll fight it. You can take that to the bank." She glared at Steve who rolled his eyes.

"I didn't say this place belongs to Ed's niece. I simply gave her permission to stay here since she was…and I quote…" He looked at her with his eyebrows raised for effect. "…short of cash."

Jennifer wasn't going to take anything Steve had to say without putting up a fuss.

"I have proof I'm his heir." She got up and returned a minute later with a faded piece of paper. "this is his will. Naming me as beneficiary. I get it all."

Betty Lou snatched the piece of paper from Jennifer's hands. "Let me see that." She scanned the document. "This is barely readable. You can't hardly even see it. I think it's a forgery." She shoved it back at Jennifer who handed it over to Steve.

"You can see for yourself. This here's my property and I want her off the land immediately. Or I'm suing…somebody."

Betty Lou huffed into another room and came back with her own piece of paper and jutted her chin up. "This here proves I'm the rightful owner of this ranch." She handed her much clearer document, and seemingly proper will, to Steve.

He nodded. "This is a will. But, we still don't know if it's the most current. You'll have to live in peace until we get this straightened out."

Steve started to switch his line of questioning when Willow coughed. "May I speak now?"

"Yes, I'm sorry. You can go now."

Willow reminded herself in this situation Steve had to be a police officer first. She brushed off her irritation at being treated as a child. She caught sight of herself in the mirror on the wall and realized she did indeed look like a child. A petulant child, but a child nonetheless. Her demeaner took on an apologetic tone rather than a combative tone. "I'm sorry I got involved in their food fight. It was not my intention, not at all. As soon as I walked in the house I was hit with more food than I could identify. One thing led to another and I, well, I couldn't just stand there and take it. I had to do something."

Steve didn't want to be having this conversation in front of Betty Lou and Jennifer so he just nodded and started questioning the ladies. He owed Willow an apology but he didn't want to embarrass her further. He knew she would have a good reason for partaking in such a juvenile stunt. Chocolate pudding dripping down his face and a probable concussion from flying apple crisp hadn't helped. He didn't waste any time getting to the heart of the matter. The one thing both murders had in common was this nasty dog fighting ring.

"Did either of you know Ed was involved in dog fighting?"

Jennifer stood up, appalled. "How would I know such a thing? I just got here. It wasn't like me and Uncle Ed were chummy or anything. I'm just his niece. To think an uncle of mine could hurt innocent, helpless dogs. How could anyone do such a thing?"

Betty Lou was much quieter.

"Betty, did you know about it?"

She nodded. This time the tears were real. "He promised me he was getting out of it. He'd made enough money and he was gonna get out before he couldn't."

"Did he ever say why he wouldn't be able to get out if he'd waited?" Steve gently asked.

"Not really. He said his partner was getting greedier. He wanted more fights. He wanted more dogs. It was almost like Ed wasn't an equal, like his partner had something on Ed and made Ed do what he wanted him to do."

"Was the partner Kelly Thomas?"

"I don't think so. She was only here for two weeks. Ed didn't know her before, I'm sure of it. He acts a certain way around new ladies. And he was all googly eyed over Kelly. Made me hoppin' mad." She quickly looked up. "You know that's true. You were here when I got home from my mama's. I didn't even know she was dead."

[114]

Steve knew what she said to be true. Unless she was a fantastic actress, and he knew she wasn't, no way she knew Kelly Thomas was dead. That doesn't mean Kelly Thomas and Ed Thomas were killed by the same person. "You may not have killed Kelly, but what was keeping you from killing Ed? You knew he'd made a fortune in dog fighting. Besides, he was flirting with Kelly Thomas. As you said before, he made you mad. Jealousy is a pretty good motive for murder. What you didn't figure on was a niece showing up and staking claim to Ed's money."

"No, I would never…I mean, I wouldn't kill Ed. I loved him."

"You couldn't produce a tear when talking about your dead boyfriend. That's an odd kind of love."

"I did love him. Like anyone else we had our problems, but I loved him." She straightened her oversized flower dress to cover up her knee-high stockings then added. "And I didn't kill him."

Steve studied her for a moment. "I think you know more than you're telling."

"No, I…" She swallowed. "He did slip up once a couple of weeks ago. Something about a guy named cubby. I'm sure it had something to do with the dogs because he clammed up as soon as he realized he was thinking out loud."

He turned to Jennifer. "What about you?"

"What about me?" She retorted.

"Perhaps you killed your uncle knowing you'd inherit the big bucks. Were you a part of his dog fighting racket?"

"I'm a member of PETA. I would never hurt an animal."

"PETA, huh? Some of those people can get pretty nasty. You might not hurt an animal, but how about a human? Especially one who was intentionally harming an animal?"

"I admit…people make me really angry. But, I wouldn't hurt anyone. Especially my uncle."

Steve stood up. "I don't want either of you going anywhere. Do you understand me?"

Both ladies mumbled, "yes."

He started for the door then turned. "And get this place cleaned up. I'll be back and if I see even one crooked picture I'm putting you both in a cell."

Willow followed, holding her black trash bag of dirty clothing. She started to speak, "I'm sorry…"

Steve put his finger to her lips then lowered his lips to hers. "Mmm…lemon meringue pie…and…pineapple jello…and barbecue chicken." He grinned. "I take it you're not hungry?"

[116]

She grinned. "Unfortunately, not much made it into my mouth. And yes, I'm starved. Can I get cleaned up first?"

"I'll drop you off then run a few errands. I'll call when I'm finished and we can meet for dinner at Molly's. I sure wish that apple cobbler hadn't ended up all over the ground."

"How is your head? Shouldn't you be seen by a doctor?"

He shook his head. "I've got a bit of a headache but I'll take some aspirin. I'll be fine."

Chapter 17

Willow let Clover out, keeping a good eye on her while she went to the bathroom. Once she was safely back inside, she climbed into the hot shower. She let the water beat down on her strained shoulders. Who knew a food fight could be such a good workout? When the water started running cooler, she climbed out and toweled off.

Clover was pacing her room and alternately barking then growling. She heard a noise outside. It seemed to be coming from the back yard. She tried to peer out the back window but the sky had already grown dark. Willow slipped on some jeans and a sweatshirt, grabbed her gun, then set off to investigate. As soon as she opened the front door Clover bolted.

"Clover, get back here. Now." The dog ignored her and disappeared around the corner of her house. Willow found Clover at the base of a tree. She was being pelted with little beads of ice. A branch had already fallen from the weight of the ice. *I really need to get a tree service out here. Some of these trees are ready to fall over.*

Convinced the weather and the cracking of limbs was all she heard, she went back inside. She highly doubted now that the dreaded freezing rain had arrived Steve would want her to drive to town. She started a fire. She really didn't feel like doing anything anyway.

She heated up some leftovers from the party for her supper. Clover was still growling by the door. "Girl. It's a storm. That's all. You're fine."

The dog insisted on going back outside, so Willow opened the door. "Have at it!"

Clover ran from view so Willow settled on the couch with her plate of meatballs, rumaki, and cucumber sandwiches. She sipped some hot apple cider and sighed. She loved her fireplace. She also loved the jacuzzi tub in her bathroom. Perhaps later she'd indulge and take a hot bath.

She took a bite of a cucumber sandwich just as a loud howl penetrated her peaceful setting. "That dog!" She opened the front door. "Clover!" The sound she heard was not Clover. She wasn't sure what it was. "Coyotes!" She ran outside to find her dog and yelled, "Clover." She heard her barking from behind the house. She only had slippers on but didn't want to take the time to put her boots on. When she arrived at the back of the house, Clover had her front paws on the same tree, barking without ceasing. "Come on girl, let's go inside."

Clover refused to budge.

Willow peered into the tree, trying to see despite the darkness. The sky was pitch black. The lack of thunder and lightning did nothing to hinder the ice though. She grabbed hold of Clover's collar and walked her to the front door. "Did you tree a squirrel? Don't you know the animals want to be in their homes with their families? You need to come inside."

She kicked off her wet slippers and cuddled back up on the couch. She took another bite.

Clover took up residence on her belly in front of the front door, a low growl emanating from her throat. Willow ignored her so she could eat. The growling turned to barking. Finally, she had had enough. "Go. Go find your squirrel. And don't expect me to come rescue you if you become an icicle. Or a frozen statue. Have you considered that, Clover?"

The dog ran out the door without bothering to answer. Willow closed it behind her saying to no one in particular, "She'll come back when she's tired of playing chase."

Once again, she sunk into her couch and picked up her plate. Her phone rang and she answered, eyeing her food as she did. She smiled. "Hey, I figured you'd be calling."

After agreeing with Steve about remaining home and staying safe, she said her goodbyes and could finally tackle her food. She heard Clover barking but chose to ignore the dog.

A loud crack made her jump. "Looks like the thunder and lightning has arrived." The dog was still barking. She opened the door as a large bolt of lightning flashed across the sky. Her eyes focused for one nanosecond on a man running across the yard with a dog behind him, nipping at his butt.

She yelled, "Clover!"

Willow ran back in the bedroom and grabbed her gun then put her slippers back on. They were better than no shoes and she didn't want to take the time to put tennis shoes on.

She ran out the front door in search of her dog and a man with a sore butt.

Willow caught up to Clover as she stood, baring her teeth, guarding the man on the ground. He was obviously in no condition to harm her since A) Clover basically had him pinned, and B) Willow had her gun pointed directly at him.

"Who are you?"

"Willow, it's me. Alex."

Willow helped Alex into the house. He was cold, bleeding and scared half to death. Even though she couldn't stand the man, she wasn't heartless. She laid some pillows on the floor in front of the fire place just as the electricity flickered then shut off. She instructed him to take his pants off and lie on his stomach while she fetched supplies. She collected her small flashlight from the kitchen and went off in search of medical supplies and candles. This time, she could not deny Clover bit him in the butt. She witnessed it with her own eyes. Of course, Alex was trespassing and Clover had every right to protect her property, at least in the state of Oklahoma.

She returned with soap and water, antibiotic ointment, and a large clean bandage. She lit some candles on the coffee table and end tables so she could see better. She gave Clover a dirty look then knelt by her ex-husband. She was just washing his bottom when the front door flew open. She must not have latched it properly when helping him in. She looked up to see Steve standing in the doorway, his fist raised obviously ready to knock. Her face turned a thousand shades of red. "Steve!"

Chapter 18

"What in the tarnation…?" Steve asked as he marched in the house and closed the door. "What is going on? Where are his pants?"

All Willow could think of saying was, "Steve, I didn't think I'd see you tonight."

"Obviously."

She sighed then asked, "What are you doing here?"

Steve repeated her question to Alex. "Yes, what are you doing here?"

Alex turned and gave Steve a devious grin.

Steve glared at Alex. He then returned the grin and asked, "What happened? That looks nasty." He came closer and studied Alex's butt. "You get bit? Gonna blame Clover again?"

Willow dumped some alcohol on Alex's wound.

Alex screamed. "Was that completely necessary?"

"I would say so. Wouldn't want you getting infected and having to go back in the hospital where you'll pull another disappearing act." She poured more on and he screamed.

"I know that wasn't necessary."

"Nope, you're right. That was for making the nurse believe I abused you when we were married."

"Oh, that. I guess I deserved it. I didn't mean it. I was just trying to get her to let me go, you know, make her feel sorry for me."

"Yeah, I got it."

She put another capful of alcohol on his butt. "Don't let it happen again."

She applied the ointment and the bandage then left while Steve helped him put Ed's sweat pants on, the same ones Willow had borrowed earlier. Once he was dressed, Willow returned.

Alex returned to the floor, stomach side down. He laid his head down on the pillow and was sleeping within ten seconds.

Willow sat on the couch. Steve joined her. They held hands. She asked, "So, back to my question. What are you doing out in this mess?"

"I was worried about you. I know you didn't prepare. I wanted to make sure you were okay."

She whispered. "That was sweet of you. I was going to call you as soon as I got him fixed up." She motioned to the snoring man on her floor. "He's lucky he only got a dog bite out of the deal. I had my gun fixed on him."

"I've got Deputy Tucker doing back ground checks on Betty Lou and Jennifer Thomas, as well as our photographer friend, Murphy McCoy, Teddy Braxton, our delivery man, and of course, Alex. Perhaps he's hiding something he shouldn't be. Let's face it, we've got more than enough on him to consider him at least a suspect for the murders. He had opportunity."

"He was in the hospital for Ed's murder."

"Are you sure? Do we know exactly what time he escaped? It'd be nice if that nurse would talk. We may march him down there, sore butt and all, to get the truth out of her. When she hears what he's been doing to dogs, and how he lied about you, maybe she'll spill all she knows. If not, I'll arrest her."

"That could work. She won't want to be marched out of her job in handcuffs. She can talk the easy way, or the hard way. Her choice."

If he's innocent of both murders we still know he's been involved in dog fighting, perhaps even breeding dogs for fighting. If convicted, he's going to see jail time." Steve paused, "Do you think Embry can handle that?"

"She won't have much of a choice. What her father has done is a horrible crime, even without the murder. She won't easily forgive him of this crime."

"I better mention, Clover really did bite him this time. I saw it with my very own eyes."

"Was Alex on your property?"

"Yep, and she was chasing him and took out a chunk of his retreating backside."

Steve chuckled. "He can't do a thing about it."

"I know. I just thought I'd better mention it."

They held hands a little while longer. "I'm going to take him in to the police station and put him in a cell. I'd hate for him to wake up and take off again. We don't need another man hunt on our hands."

She stood up and looked outside. "Are you sure you want to risk it? It's a mess out there."

"Yeah. I need to be accessible in case of an emergency. We'll be fine. I've got chains on the truck tires and I'll take my time."

"I really don't think he'll be able to sit on his backside anytime soon. I think you should wait out the storm here. I've got a small backup generator that my grandfather kept around so we can keep our phones charged. If you can get it started. You'll be accessible and safe. What do you think of that?"

"Hmm…I don't like the idea of spending the night here. A single woman…"

"Steve. It's an emergency. Unless you're going to call an ambulance to transport him, or put him on his stomach in the back of your truck, I don't think leaving is going to work."

He sighed and looked down at the still snoring form in front of the fireplace. "I suppose you're right. And I don't feel comfortable leaving him here with you all alone. My only choice is camping out here on the couch. I'll keep the fire going." He kissed her. "You better take Clover in with you…she'll help keep you warm."

Chapter 19

Willow realized they were without heat, but darn, it got cold overnight. The sun was just coming up. She had some day-old pastries from the coffee shop. That'd have to do them until they got some electric back. Although, if Steve got that generator going she could use that to generate enough electricity to make coffee. "Coffee." She said aloud, dreaming about something hot and rich and… "What am I doing torturing myself like this? Steve probably didn't even get it started." She slipped on her slippers over her stockinged feet. She wore sweats and a sweatshirt to bed. Clover was pacing, needing to go outside. She put her fuzzy robe over her sweats and listened at the bedroom door. Nothing. Not a sound. "Huh." I'll just let Clover out the back door so she doesn't wake them.

Clover dropped right outside the door then wanted back in. She hated getting her paws cold. Willow had to coax her outside just to go once she saw the ground covered in ice. "You are spoiled." Willow wiped her paws off with a towel and the dog climbed back up in bed. Willow pet her then said, "I'm just gonna peek at the guys. I'll be right back."

Willow walked lightly down the hall and peeked around the corner of the living room. The fire was out. Steve was still sitting on the couch but straight as an arrow. Willow glanced to the empty pillows on the floor and she filled with dread. She ran to Steve who was thankfully still alive, mad, but alive. He was tied up with extension cords, several by the look of it. His feet were tied, his hands were tied, and his arms were tied down to his body. She noticed his gun was missing and a note on the table.

She read out loud. "Sorry, but my life is at stake. I'll ditch the truck on the side of the road along with the keys to your jeep and your cellphones. Again, I'm sorry. I wouldn't do this if there was any other way."

Willow looked up when she heard Steve grunting. "Oh sheesh, what was I thinking?" She ripped the tape off his mouth and at the same times asked, "What did you say?"

Steve screamed. "I said go slow."

She looked down at the facial hair attached to the duct tape and the rectangle patch of bare skin on his face. "Oh. I'm sorry. You're gonna have to…never mind. I'll untie you." She was going to mention he'd have to shave but thought it best she didn't say anything. He'd know as soon as he looked in a mirror.

Willow worked to free Steve of all the cords while he was explaining what happened. Apparently, Alex managed to get the drop on him. Steve had been working on the generator, which he never did get running, and when he came back Alex was waiting for him with a knife. He proceeded to take his gun as well as the knife he kept strapped to his leg.

"You keep a knife on your leg? How did I not know this?"

Steve shook his head. "Probably because you've never seen my bare legs."

Willow said, "Huh. You're right. I haven't." She continued. "So, he took your gun and tied you up?"

"Yep, said if I screamed he'd have to tie you up too and probably shoot the dog. I figured you'd be up eventually. Who knows how long it would take someone to get out here if we were both tied up. Especially with the ice. So, I thought it best to keep my mouth shut. We'll get him."

Willow grimaced. "I don't have a house phone. Got rid of it after I moved in."

"We're gonna have to walk to the neighbors to call for help. I'm guessin' they'll have some hot coffee ready too. Probably not the stuff you're used to but it will be hot and that's pretty much all we can ask for at this point."

"Sounds good to me. Just let me get dressed."

Fifteen minutes later the pair set off for Willow's nearest neighbor.

"You know it's about a half mile, right?"

"Yep."

She was taking baby steps to keep from falling to her bottom. "And at this rate, it's going to take us hours."

"Yep."

"You don't have much to say, do you?"

His look was answer enough.

She raised her eyebrows and clamped her mouth shut. He was cleanly shaven. Having to shave put him in an even worse mood than he already was. She wasn't the one who put tape across his mouth. She'd hate to be Alex when they found him.

Willow fell a total of six times, which she didn't think was too bad since every single footfall was on ice. Everything was coated in it—road, gravel, weeds, grass...everything. Steve didn't fall once. She wondered if he was a closet Yankee.

What seemed like forever later they arrived at the front door of a lovely two-story farm house. Willow noticed immediately, the lights were on.

Which was a good indication, there would be coffee.

The elderly rancher recognized Steve right away. "Chief. Everyone's been wonderin' where you'd got yourself off to. I even rode by Willow's place but there weren't no cars so I didn't think anybody was home. What you doin' out here in the cold?" He motioned for them to come in while he was talking. "The missus has coffee ready. She'll whip up some breakfast too. You're lookin' mighty cold."

Steve quickly explained what happened then asked the rancher why everyone was looking for him.

"Well, there was an accident of sorts. Out at Ed's place. Those two women stayin' there were cryin' and raisin' a fuss like you wouldn't believe. Says someone was out there, tryin' to get in the place. Betty Lou had to use the shot gun to get em to leave the house alone. Only thing was, he went for the garage. He burnt it clean down. Not sure why someone'd do such a thing, but that barn is gone. Good thing all the critters were taken out of there." He took a couple of mugs out of the cabinet and poured them each a cup of dark brew. "Sugar? Cream?"

Willow shook her head and took a sip. "Nope. Black is perfect. Thank you."

Steve took his cup and used the rancher's cell phone to make some calls. "Deputy Tucker will be here as soon as he can. It's going to take him a little while to get out here though. Not only was Ed's barn set on fire, but we've got downed power lines all over the county. Just getting around felled trees and branches is going to take some time, let alone dealing with the ice."

Willow peered out the kitchen window. The walk had been a little too tense to enjoy the beauty all around her. The heavy branches were glistening with ice. Every direction she looked white crosses stared back at her…brilliant diamonds. She nearly held her breath.

"Did you hear me?"

Willow turned toward Steve. "Yes, help is on the way." She smiled at him then turned toward outside. "Isn't it beautiful?"

Steve took a few seconds to see the view through her eyes. "Yes, creation always amazes me." He took a drink. "I believe breakfast is ready. We might as well eat while we're waiting."

Willow sat down to a hearty breakfast of eggs, bacon, sausage gravy and homemade biscuits.

The rancher's wife smiled. "I had almost everything already done. Just had to add a few more eggs to the bowl. My motto is always be prepared to feed an unexpected guest. Besides, leftover breakfast for lunch is always a treat. Frees up my afternoon for quiltin'."

Willow devoured her breakfast and was surprised when a pan of cinnamon rolls appeared on the table. She rubbed her stomach. "I shouldn't but…" She took a large roll and doused it in butter. The flaky pastry nearly melted in her mouth. "Have you ever thought about making these to sell? I would put them in the coffee shop."

The woman laughed and put her hands to her face. "Oh my. Why, I never gave it a thought. I'll have to think on that."

Deputy Tucker knocked on the door. "Ma'am." He said as he eyed the rolls.

"Deputy, be sure to take one of these rolls with you. You can eat it on the drive."

His grin puffed out his cheeks. "Yes, Ma'am. I will, Ma'am."

She handed him a small paper plate with a cinnamon roll.

Sheriff Tucker spoke quietly for the Chief's ears only. Afterward, Steve said, "Willow, I think it might be best if you stayed at your place. I'll come get you as soon as it's safe. We've got a lot of work to do before I'll be getting to looking for my truck. I don't want you sitting in a patrol car for hours in the cold."

"Yeah, I might be more productive at home. I can get a fire going and perhaps grill up some food for later. You'll be hungry after working all day."

The rancher piped up. "I'll run her home in a bit. She might as well stay here and keep warm for a while. Besides, in a few hours all the ice'll be melted. Safer to drive then."

Steve left Willow in the capable hands of the rancher and his wife.

Chapter 20

Several hours later Willow found herself lounging in front of the fire with Clover. Instead of leftovers, she'd been served a wonderful vegetable beef soup and a big slice of homemade bread with fresh churned butter. "Clover, you missed out. I need a personal chef. I really do." She pat the dog's head. "You seem awfully tired. What have you been doing since I left?"

Clover just groaned a little and rested her head on Willow's chest. She had let the dog out as soon as she arrived home and Clover seemed fine then. Since, she'd grown lethargic. Willow stood and got the dog a treat. She loved her treats. The dog didn't move. Something was wrong.

Willow ran for the front door and opened it to find the veterinarian, Doctor Drake standing on the threshold. "Oh my gosh. Talk about perfect timing. My dog, Clover. Something's wrong. Please, look at her. She's not normally like this."

He smiled. "I'll be happy to. Lead the way." He knelt next to Clover and opened his bag. He pulled out a gun and pointed it at Willow. "Thank you for inviting me. Your husband has something of mine and I want it back. I'm guessing it's here."

"Ex-husband." Willow glanced around the room, trying to come up with a plan. "And I have no idea what you're talking about."

"An envelope. A large manila envelope. Did he give it to you for safe keeping?" He motioned for her to sit down. "I knew Alex would come here. Too bad that cop friend of yours stuck around. I figured I could handle you and Alex, but, I'm a smart man…and patient." He glanced at the sleeping dog. "Your dog had a nice snack outside. I haven't met a dog yet that could resist a good steak. If you give a dog enough Benadryl she'll be out for the count for quite a while. We shouldn't be hearing from Clover for quite some time. Maybe never." He shook his head. "I wasn't quite sure of her weight so I had to guess on how much to give her. I could have overdone it." He shrugged. "The sacrifices one makes when plans go haywire."

"You drugged my dog? What kind of vet are you?" Willow was disgusted. The guy had given her the creeps the first time she'd met him. She needed to learn to trust her gut more.

"A bad vet. A very bad vet. Now, enough small talk. Where is my envelope?"

"I really have no idea what you're talking about. It's not like Alex and I were close. We barely tolerated one another."

He grunted. "Fine. Have it your way." He pulled some zip ties from his bag and secured her feet and hands. "I'll do a thorough search. I don't need your help. You can just sit here, relax, and watch me go through everything you own."

Willow felt violated. He was tearing books off shelves, emptying drawers, touching all her stuff. "If you tell me what's in the envelope maybe I'll have an idea of where he put it. If it's here at all."

He laughed. An evil glance landed on her. "I guess it won't matter now. You'll have to have an unfortunate accident after I find the envelope." He dumped out a kitchen drawer. "Money. Pictures. Ledgers. Pretty much everything that could put me away for a very long time. Ed wanted out. Did you know that?" He dumped another drawer. "He said he'd had a change of heart. I thought if I used his full legal name and sent him candy laced with poison, no one would put two and two together. My plan was to frame Alex. But, no, that didn't work out to plan either. That bimbo just happened to share a name with Ed." He opened the hall closet and started pulling out boxes.

"Kelly Thomas. We called her Cubby. I had no idea they shared the same name. Cubby who provided pit bull pups for underground fight clubs all over the US. Who would have guessed she shared a name with a fat Santa wanna be?" He emptied another box. "Good thing I already got my dogs from her. No worries. I'll find someone else to provide dogs if these four don't work out. In my line of business greedy people are everywhere."

"So, you really meant to kill Ed, not Kelly. Or Cubby, or whatever her name was."

"Ladies and Gentlemen, she's catching on."

Willow had no idea who he thought he was talking to. She was beginning to think he was crazy. "So, it was you who ordered the chocolate using Alex's phone. When did you do that?" She figured if she could keep him talking long enough someone might come to her aid.

"Child's play, my dear. I'm very good at taking things. Never leave your phone lying around." He held up a phone. "I have Deputy Tucker's girlfriend's phone too. It's amazing how distracting a cute puppy can be." He laughed again.

A chill went through Willow as the reality of Ed's death hit her. "You weren't just arriving at

Ed's that night. You were just leaving. You had just killed him!"

"I've heard you're pretty smart. I really expected more from you. I guess you've been distracted having your ex back in town. I'm sure your pretty daughter's wedding has stolen some of your attention as well. Let's hope that envelope is here, or else I'm gonna have to pay your daughter a visit."

Willow's heart began to race. She had to protect her daughter. "So, you're the one who signed Alex out of the hospital?"

"Ding ding ding. She's right again. You are batting a thousand."

"Why didn't you get the envelope from him then?"

"At that point, I thought Alex and I could still do business together. I figured he'd be taking over his girlfriend's business and no harm done. I guess I thought wrong."

It was Willow's turn to laugh. "Alex has never had a motivated bone in his body. You really thought he'd be ambitious enough to raise dogs? He can't even take care of himself."

He ignored her comments and continued. "I got him out of the hospital and took him to Ed's. He said he was gonna shower and get cleaned up, then we'd have to get out of there before the police chief was knocking on Ed's door. I heard the shower running and figured he was on the up and up. After a half hour, I figured something was up and went in after him. The scum climbed out the bathroom window and took off. First, he let the air out of my tires then he had the audacity to call me to tell me to stay away from you and Embry. He had a whole envelope of evidence against me and if anything happened to the two of you, he'd give it to the authorities. Oh yeah, he took my money too. Ed and I were partners so any money Ed had was rightfully mine. He must have hitchhiked to your house. I guessed right away where he was going. He didn't know anyone else. He and Cubby thought it was a great front for selling dogs in this area…being here for your daughter's engagement party. I bet they didn't even give her a gift, did they?"

He turned her entire living room and kitchen upside down and didn't find a thing. He grinned. "Looks like I'm gonna have to spend some time in your bedroom. Maybe after I find what I'm looking for we can enjoy a little romp before you say goodbye to this world. Go out with a bang, huh?"

Willow despised the sound of his wicked laugh. If she could, she'd put a bullet in his heart and end it forever, she would. Unfortunately, her gun was in the bedroom. He would soon taunt her with it, she was sure. He disappeared. She heard her drawers hitting the bedroom floor and she cringed. If she got out of this she'd have to buy all new underclothes. Knowing he touched her things made her sick to her stomach. She heard a sound behind her and she twisted her head to see Alex walk in.

Her eyes grew big and he put his finger to his lips, hushing her. He pulled Steve's gun out of his waistband and waited for the vet to walk back in the living room.

She heard approaching footsteps and turned her focus back to Clover. She didn't want to alert Doctor Drake to Alex's presence.

"The bedroom was a bust. Hopefully the guest room or office turn up the goods. Otherwise, we're gonna have to skip that romp. I'm sure Embry will be…"

"I told you what would happen if you came anywhere near Willow or Embry."

Willow's whole body froze. As long as she was with Alex she had never heard him speak with such a serious, matter of fact tone. She watched Doctor Drake's mouth stop moving. He slowly turned, reaching for his gun.

"I wouldn't do that if I were you." Alex pointed his gun directly at the doctor's chest.

Dr. Drake struggled with which direction to go. Do as Alex instructed or go for the gun. He decided Alex didn't have it in him and his hand flew for his waistband where he'd put Willow's little revolver.

Alex fired two shots and the doctor fell backward.

Willow screamed then passed out.

Chapter 21

Willow woke up to find her hands and feet freed from their constraints. "Am I...was I having a nightmare?"

Steve was holding her head. "No, Honey, you weren't dreaming. Doctor Drake is dead. Alex is at the police station." He wiped her forehead. "Embry is on her way. Everything is going to be okay."

She sat up and looked at the stained spot on her floor. "I can't stay here, Steve. I can't wake up to that every day."

He held her. "I've got a plan. My sister has that apartment we had dinner in. You'll stay there and I'll make sure this place gets the remodel you've been wanting. I'll take care of everything. Just trust me."

She laid her head back on his lap. "How did I get so lucky to have you in my life?"

"I think we're both blessed to have each other."

She was silent for a minute. "He planned on killing me, Steve." She began to panic. "Then he was going to hurt Embry. Alex isn't going to be charged with murder, is he?"

"Alex is not being charged with murder. The doctor's death was self-defense, plain and simple. Alex will have to answer for his part in the dog fighting ring, whatever that may be, but I have a feeling the judge is going to go easy on him because he chose to come here and make sure you and his daughter were safe. That took guts. Especially from a guy who tends to run from responsibility."

Willow nodded. "Yes, he was brave. I've never heard him sound so resolute. It was like he had come to terms with the fact he may die trying to save us. There was no fear. No humor. No compromise. He didn't flinch when it came time to fire the gun. He just did what had to be done." She settled back down then said, "I need a vacation."

***

A week later Willow was watching the foal run around the round pen, waiting on Embry who decided she wanted horseback riding lessons. Steve pulled up to give her an update on the house.

She smiled as she listened to him talk about new drywall and flooring. He was enjoying the remodel. Even if he was still in demolition mode.

Perhaps that was why he was enjoying the project so much. A wall can be a great thing to take one's frustration out on. He then told her Doctor Drake wasn't even a veterinarian. He was a fake. She listened to him go on about the case and how Alex got off with probation since he'd never profited from any of the dog fighting. He promised he'd come back for the wedding but Willow was doubtful that would happen.

Once he quieted down, Willow pulled out an envelope and handed it to Steve.

"What's this?"

"I've had this in my purse since Valentine's Day.

He opened his card. There was a large red foil heart on the front with the question, do you know what I love about you? Inside simply read, "Everything!"

He grinned. "I thought, I mean, you never said…"

She smiled. "I never said I love you back, did I? I was going to, then we got distracted and well, I'm saying it now." She kissed him. "I love you, Steve Grice."

He sighed. "Woman, it's about time. Ever since our picnic I've wondered…well, I just wasn't sure…"

She hushed him with her kiss.

"Willow's" Appetizer Meatballs

(Original recipe was posted in 1989 in Taste of Home. Embry has loved them ever since!)

Meatballs

- 2 lbs lean ground beef
- 1 lb pork sausage
- 1 (5 oz) can evaporated milk
- 2 cups old fashioned oats
- ½ tsp ground pepper
- 2 tsp chili powder
- ½ tsp garlic powder
- 2 tsp salt
- 2 eggs
- ½ cup chopped onions

Sauce

- 4 cups catsup
- 3 cups brown sugar
- 2 tsp liquid smoke
- 1 tsp garlic powder
- 1 cup chopped onions

Mix meatball ingredients together then shape into 1 inch balls. Place in baking pan in a single layer and pour sauce over them. Bake at 350 degrees for 1 hour.

Willow's Cucumber sandwiches

Ingredients:

- Mini bagels
- 8 oz softened Cream Cheese
- ½ cup mayonnaise
- 1 Envelope of Italian dressing mix
- Dill
- Thinly sliced cucumber

Mix cream cheese, mayonnaise, and Italian dressing together. Spread on bagel halves. Top with cucumber slices. Sprinkle with dill

Willow & Embry's Rumaki

Willow and Embry created their own rumaki using a simple combination of bacon, water chestnuts, and pineapple. Dipped in their homemade ginger sauce, these little bites can't be beat at a party.

- Bacon
- Sliced water chestnuts
- 20 oz Pineapple chunks (reserve liquid)
- Toothpicks

Cut bacon slices in thirds. Wrap one piece of pineapple and one water chestnut in bacon. Secure with a toothpick. Bake at 400 degrees until bacon crisps, about ten minutes. Serve alongside ginger sauce.

Willow & Embry's Ginger Sauce

- Reserved pineapple juice
- ¼ cup soy sauce
- 1/8 cup rice wine vinegar
- 1/8 cup white wine
- ¾ cup brown sugar
- 2 TBS cornstarch
- 1 ½ tsp ginger
- ¼ tsp salt

Mix cornstarch, pineapple juice, and soy sauce. Add remaining ingredients. Cook until thick and bubbly, stirring constantly. Remove from heat and cool slightly. If making ahead, cover sauce with plastic wrap to keep a film from developing. Serve with rumaki or ham.

Willow's Sausage Gravy

Enjoy on your favorite biscuits. (Willow uses Pillsbury because every time she makes homemade they end up like bricks. The gravy can't be beat though…she gets raves about it anytime she takes it anywhere.)

- 1 pound bacon
- 12 oz roll of pork sausage
- ½ cup flour
- 4 ½ cups whole milk
- Salt
- Pepper

Fry one pound of bacon. Remove bacon reserving grease. Crumble sausage into bacon grease and fry until no longer pink. Remove sausage, reserving bacon grease. Using a whisk, reduce heat and slowly whisk flour into grease until a roux. When all flour has been incorporated into oil, continue stirring with whisk for an additional minute. This removes the flour taste from the gravy. Slowly pour milk into roux.

Bring mixture to a slow boil. If gravy is too thick once it hits the boiling point, add a little more milk until desired consistency is achieved. Once gravy is at desired thickness, turn off the heat and add sausage, salt and pepper to taste to the mixture.

Please enjoy this excerpt from 'Cruisin' for a Bruisin'', Book 7 of the Willow Crier Cozy Mystery Series

Chapter 1

Willow heard her name yelled before she saw the group she was supposed to be with. She looked around and spotted Harry, her grandfather's best friend, yelling her name. Had her grandfather still been living he would have been right next to Harry.

Harry was waving frantically trying to get her attention. She waved back. "Embry," she said nervously, "do you see what I see?" Harry wore an oversize hat and his face, arms and legs were smothered in sunscreen. The real kicker was the large pink flamingo floatie he was wearing around his mid-section.

Embry nodded. "Mom, what have we agreed to?"

She and Embry took a one-way flight to Houston a few days before their cruise embarked so they could shop for wedding dresses. Now, it was time to check in for their cruise. The lines were atrocious. "Honey, I needed a vacation. We wanted to spend some time together before your wedding. The opportunity presented itself to travel with the assisted living center, at a great deal, I might add, so we jumped on it." She sighed. "We'll survive."

Embry shrugged and joined the seniors who were all loud and rambunctious. Harry, being the loudest of them all.

Once the group was able to check in their luggage, the long wait in the security line began. Willow noticed there were two lines. "Why can't we go in that line? It's moving a lot faster?" She joined the fast-moving line.

A cruise line employee greeted her. "May I help you?"

"What do I have to do to go through security this way?"

"This line is for suite guests. Did you book a suite with us?"

"Well, I have a balcony. That's not considered a suite, is it?"

The worked smiled, apologetically. "I'm sorry, but no. There's always next time."

Willow rejoined her group then said, "It was a bust."

Embry just pointed to the sign that clearly stated the line was for crown members and suite guests.

Willow shrugged. "It was worth a try."

Two hours later, after Harry received angry glances from more than one fellow cruiser for hitting them with his pink flamingo as he turned in line, they arrived at the security gates.

Harry didn't want to part with his flamingo. Security wouldn't let him pass with it attached to his body so he had no choice but to relinquish the thing. His shoulders visibly sagged.

"Harry, you'll be able to re-inflate it. Don't worry."

"I didn't bring my air pump and I can't blow it up."

Willow reassured him. "We'll figure it out. Come on, this is supposed to be a fun time. Tell you what, after we eat lunch and get into our rooms, I'll go swimming with you and the gang. I'll even go down the waterslide with you."

At this news Harry perked up. "Okay. After lunch. It's a date. Don't forget!" He cautioned her.

"Harry, I promise I won't forget. I'm all yours for the afternoon."

Harry and his buddies had three connecting interior rooms. Their plan was to not spend any time in their cabins but to sleep. He scooted off to join his buddies in checking out their rooms.

Once everyone checked in, Willow glanced around to find she was alone with Embry. "Want to take advantage of the alone time and grab some lunch?"

Embry's stomach growled. "I'd say that is a yes."

The found a corner booth and ducked in with their plates. When they were finished, and sipping on their ice tea, a waiter leaned on a banister directly to Willow's right. She overheard his conversation. "Did you send the package?" Silence. "I haven't got it yet." Silence. "Okay, I'll let you know when it arrives." She raised her eyebrows at Embry.

The waiter realized he'd been heard and quickly explained. "My mother. She sends me packages." He nervously told them to have a wonderful cruise then left.

Willow shrugged. "He seems a little old to be getting packages from home. But, to each his own. Want dessert?"

"Mom, we've already had dessert."

"Oh. Okay." The café was on the 14th floor of the ship and had panoramic views of the city of Galveston. She glanced at her watch. "It's after 1.

Our room should be ready. Should we go check it out?"

Embry grinned. "You bet!"

Sure enough, their sailaway card opened the door. Willow went straight for the balcony. "Embry, you've got to see this!" She stood at the balcony railing and pointed toward the water. "Dolphins. Can you believe it?"

At four o'clock the ship sounded its horn and started pulling away from the pier. "Can you believe it, Mom? We're going out into the ocean!"

As the two of them explored all the nooks and crannies of the room, there was a knock on the door. Embry said, "Probably our luggage. I'll get it."

Willow heard the door open, Embry yell, and the door slam followed by a very demanding, "Mother!"

Willow jumped up and hurried to the door. "What is it? What happened?"

"Just open the door."

Willow shrugged. "Okay." She opened the door. Nothing could have prepared her for what stood before her. Harry, in all his nearly naked glory, nearly glowing for the coat of sunscreen, skin sagging in places she really never, ever even thought existed, was grinning ear to ear in nothing but a speedo. Words failed her.

[159]

"Are you ready? You don't even have your suit on yet."

"Um, um…I see you managed to get your flamingo blown back up." She refused to let her eyes wander any farther down than the pink ring around his protruding middle. Once was more than enough. The man was tall. And a bean pole. Except his stomach.

"Yeah, Jack brought a twin air mattress and a pump. Just in case. He's got a bad back. Besides, the guys brought their swim toys too."

That's when she noticed Jack and Harold standing to either side of Harry. Both also in speedos. Both covered in sunscreen. Thankfully, they were carrying their various pool toys rather than wearing them. What could she say? "Alright guys, let me change. I'll be right out."

She closed the door and turned to find Embry still standing with her mouth hanging open closed it long enough to say, "There are just some things you can never un-see."

A Yankee's Guide to Southern Phrases

Bless Your Heart: The most back handed kind words spoken in the south. Means, while you're sweet, you're also stupid, you don't quite get it and I feel sorry for you.

Fixin to: About to do something, almost ready, thinking about doing something.

Nervous as a long tail cat in a room full of rockin' chairs: Nervous to the point of being jumpy.

Reckon: So suppose or believe something is true.

Yankee: Anyone originating north of the Mason Dixon line.

Redneck: Polite, blue collar individual who loves hunting, country music, and blue jeans. Add alcohol and anything can happen.

Y'all: You guys

All y'all: More than five people

I could eat the north end of a south-bound polecat: Starving!

Lil' Dogie: A motherless calf, a calf separated from its cow.

Hankering: Craving something

Fair to middlin': Doing okay

Three sheets to the wind: Drunker than a skunk

Passel: A whole bunch

Hold your horses: Be patient

Grinning like a possum eating a sweet potato: Happy as can be

He's a snake in the grass: Mean as all get out

Gussied Up: Dressed fancy

Halfcocked: Acting on assumptions or partial information. Based on old firearms, that if not fully cocked (thus halfcocked), would not fire.

Barkin' up the wrong tree: Misguided, mistaken

Kicked the bucket: Died

See all the way to Christmas: Skirt so short you can see what you shouldn't be seeing.

Hodunk: backwoods town with no value

Author Bio

Lilly York? (aka Darlene Shortridge, author of Contemporary Christian Fiction) How about Lilly Belle; a mis-plant northerner, living in a southern world. Southern charm is lost among late nights with a two year old granddaughter, heat flashes competing with hell, copious re-runs of Murder She Wrote with Jessica Fletcher catching the bad guy, and a vivid imagination keeping insanity at bay.

In both humor and mystery, Lilly draws inspiration from terrible twos, a 24 year old daughter who questions her sanity, a son who constantly spews bad puns, and a husband who has selective hearing. Though, that's perfectly alright with her, because what can you love more than a good laugh and a family so dysfunctional they almost seem functional?

To stay informed on the whereabouts and goings-on of the Willow Crier Cozy Mystery Characters as well as upcoming releases, recipes and maybe a clue or two, join Lilly's e-mail club by going to…

LillyYork.com

Get your free short story!

Grandpa Goes Missing

Find out what happened to bring Willow down to
Oklahoma in the first place.
Be the first in line to read Lilly York's latest books, get
extra recipes from Willow's kitchen, get 'sneak peeks'
on works-in-progress, receive special offers and so
much more…
FREE short story only available here!

www.lillyyork.com/shortstory

Get yours today!